ADOPTED MIRACLES

Anamika Mukherjee has spent over a decade in the field of communication and publishing. She began her career as a leisure and lifestyle journalist in Delhi, then transitioned smoothly to website content writer, then to instructional designer and currently she works as a technical writer in Bangalore. Her first book, *Worth Every Gasp* (Prakash Books, 2011), tells the tales of her adventures while trekking solo in the western Himalayas.

In addition to writing, she enjoys travel, photography, playing tennis and going shopping with her girls.

ADOPTED MIRACLES

The Story of Our Family

ANAMIKA MUKHERJEE

HarperCollins *Publishers* India

First Published in India in 2014 by
HarperCollins *Publishers* India

Building 10, Tower A, 4th Floor, DLF Cyber City, Phase II,
Gurugram Haryana – 122002, India
www.harpercollins.co.in

ISBN: 978-93-5029-787-2

2 4 6 8 10 9 7 5 3 1

Typeset in 12/15 Dante MT by
R. Ajith Kumar

Printed and bound at
MicroPrints India, New Delhi

To my two lovely daughters
who are everything I ever hoped for ... and more

Contents

Prologue

It is difficult to say when, exactly, the story of our long journey to have a family began. For many people, the story begins with getting married, so in a way that is an appropriate place to start.

We got married relatively young – at twenty-four. Amit was my 'childhood sweetheart'. Not childhood exactly, considering we were sixteen when we met. Sweet sixteen. Ours was in many ways a clichéd romance – literally the boy / girl next door. We were neighbours for a few months, then we were in different cities for all the intervening years till we got married. It was before the era of mobile phones and email. It was, in fact, the era when STD phone calls were an expensive affair, not to be taken lightly. Still, we kept in touch through all the ups and downs of our student lives. And one fine day, when we both were twenty-three, on one of our rare-but-long long-distance conversations, I asked him if he'd like to marry me.

I didn't actually mean that we should get married right away, but once he'd agreed (and it wasn't all that easy getting him to agree), there didn't seem to be any good reason to defer the matter. Parents, who had been aware of our long-distance romance all along, were roped into the discussion and – though somewhat surprised at this turn of events – agreed happily. Before we knew quite what we were getting into, the date was set and invitations were being printed. Oops – too late to change our minds now!

That was back in 1998.

We hadn't talked too much about starting a family back then. We both vaguely assumed that – some day – we would want to. But we were twenty-four – much too young to consider the matter seriously and much too happy just being a family of two.

When I turned thirty, six years later, it suddenly struck me that if I ever wanted to have kids, I'd better start working on it. Soon.

It also became suddenly quite clear to me that I did want to have kids. Kids, mind you: not one, but two. At least two. In my mind, suddenly, life without kids was not an option, and just as surely, one was a lonely number. I wasn't aware of when exactly these convictions took root, but when I started to consciously think about kids as my thirtieth birthday loomed, I discovered that they were already firmly in place.

Amit, on the other hand, had decided in the intervening years that two was a pretty good number. We were two already. Why did we need anyone else? He didn't want to have kids, he said. Not now. Not ever.

I kept thinking that, given time, he would change his mind. He was clearly just confused. He didn't want the added responsibility, he wasn't ready to give up his freedom, he was still young. But he'd come around, some day. He was such terribly good 'father' material. He loved kids – much more so than I ever did.

But Amit didn't come around. As I began to think more and more about having a family, I became more and more painfully aware that I was alone in my dreams. We began to discuss the matter more often, and we realized that this gap between us could never be bridged. So irreconcilable did it seem that I decided it was time for us to split.

So we split. For three months, we stayed separately and met only occasionally. Amit thought our marriage was over; I hadn't made up my mind. It was a very tough time for both of us – made no easier by parents on both sides getting involved. Friends also knew – and though they tried their best to be supportive and take no sides, it was awkward. And lonely.

In the end, we decided to work things out. Amit was forced to face his demons and work out why he didn't want to have kids. Slowly and painfully, we uncovered the reasons behind his reluctance, and tried to resolve the matter to everyone's satisfaction. It took months, maybe even years, but eventually we managed to put our marriage back together again and started to plan our family.

It was October 2004, and I was already over thirty. Still, we had just time enough to squeeze in two babies before I hit thirty-five – and all the ageing problems associated with it.

So, in October 2004, I thought our troubles were over ... but they were just beginning.

ONE

Trying to Conceive

I

Getting a marriage back on track after a serious breach is not an easy task. Things continued to be rocky between the two of us for a while, so it wasn't really surprising that a year later we still had no 'good news' to tell friends and family.

If it wasn't surprising, it still *was* worrying. We'd stopped the contraceptives, and I'd been keeping track of my dates. We'd been consciously working on having sex at the right time of the month. Something should have worked out by now. Reluctantly, without really being convinced that I needed to, I went to see a gynaecologist. I had not needed a gynae much so far, and I didn't have a regular one, so I just walked into a clinic near home. With some awkwardness, I stated my problem.

'My husband and I have been trying to conceive for the last year or so, but it hasn't happened.'

'Your periods are regular?' asked the doctor in a bored tone.

'Yes, fairly regular – though I have a five-week cycle. Actually it varies from about thirty to about thirty-three, thirty-four days.'

'And you have regular relations with your husband?'

This stumped me. Of course I had a regular relationship with my husband. We had been living under the same roof for so many years, hadn't we? Or did she mean relations as in relatives? But then, what could that possibly mean? I must have looked dazed, because she repeated the question impatiently, this time in a slightly suggestive manner, with the slightest emphasis on the word 'relations'. That's when the penny dropped.

I assured her we had a sufficiently active sex life, but she only lectured me about the female cycle, the importance of having 'relations' and told me to be patient. 'Come back after two years,' she said dismissively, and I went away with my tail between my legs.

It was almost a year later that I summoned up the courage to consult another gynaecologist. It wasn't an easy decision – by then, it was pretty clear that something *was* wrong, and that the 'have sex and leave it to Nature' approach just wasn't working.

It hadn't been an easy year. What had started off as a

fairly casual attempt to get pregnant had turned increasingly desperate – at least on my part. In the early days of trying to conceive, I'd just gone off the pill and hoped that some day we'd get lucky. As the months went by and I started keeping track of my dates and having sex – or forcing us to have sex – on the days around ovulation, the tension built up, both in me and in our relationship. I started reading up on the Internet to make sure that whatever I remembered from my tenth standard biology class was not too far off the mark. It wasn't, but the Internet did give me some tips I'd never known about before – especially about correctly identifying the time of ovulation. Some were simple but tedious, like charting your basal body temperature for a few months to be able to predict the day it would be lowest. Somehow, taking one's temperature every morning before even fully waking up didn't sound like much fun. Other suggestions were even less appealing. One website suggested keeping track of the position of the cervix. Another suggested checking the quantity and slipperiness of one's vaginal discharge. Charming.

In the end, I realized that the mild twinges of pain in my lower abdomen that troubled me for a few hours every so often were all I needed to know exactly when I was ovulating.

The more I read about understanding the signs, counting the days, planning the intercourse, the more I wondered why it wasn't working for us; we were already doing everything right. Interest and curiosity slowly grew into a full-fledged obsession.

Initially, I'd been only the tiniest bit disappointed when my period announced its arrival every month. Back then, I knew it was only a matter of waiting and trying, patience and persistence. I didn't know anything about infertility in those days. It was just something that happened to other people.

As the months rolled by, my hope – even conviction – that this time we'd get lucky, this time we'd nail it, *this* would be the time we'd finally have the fantastic, exciting news to share with our friends and family grew stronger. And every month, the disappointment hit me that much harder.

II

Why is it that when you desperately want something, all you can see around you are people who already have it? Years earlier, I remember, when I was looking for a job, all I could see around me were other young women leaving for office early in the morning, returning late in the evening, smiling, tired, satisfied. If they could find a job, why couldn't I?

It was the same thing now. Everywhere I turned, I saw

pregnant women, or mothers with infants. There they were, women with enormous bumps, babies in strollers, colleagues in office going on maternity leave, or those with children always talking about them, sharing stories of pregnancy, labour, delivery, school admissions, illnesses – all those things that I longed to share, but couldn't because, damn it, I couldn't even get pregnant.

Luckily, because Amit and I had married early, many of our friends who had married later had not yet had babies. We had a good circle of friends in Bangalore. We were particularly close to two other couples whom we'd known for years: Sridhar and Sowmya, and Vyom and Vipra. Amit had known Vyom practically from the cradle, and they had been classmates and room-mates in engineering college. I had first met Vyom back in Delhi, even before Amit and I had decided to get married. It was a most interesting experience. Vyom had recently got a job and moved to Delhi, and Amit, who was already working in Bangalore, put us in touch with each other. After we had spoken to each other on the phone a few times, we set up a blind date with each other outside PVR in Vasant Vihar. This was in the days when only the most elite and pretentious people actually had mobile phones.

'How will we recognize each other?' I asked.

'I've seen a photo of you. Amit had it on him in hostel.'

I knew that photo – there was only one, or at best two photos, that we had of each other. What Vyom had seen was a dim, blurred print from some very old and shaky camera. It had been taken when I was sixteen, which was already many years ago. If memory served, I had long hair in that photograph and I wasn't wearing my glasses. If Amit had, in fact, been in the habit of taking the print out and gazing fondly at it from time to time in the intervening years, it was no doubt a great deal the worse for wear.

'You really think you can recognize me from that?' I asked sceptically.

Vyom, however, didn't think it would be too much of a problem. 'I'll be wearing a green shirt, you'll be able to find me by that. And I'm sure I'll recognize you. Don't worry, we'll find each other.'

Neither of us had any idea just how many men wearing green shirts could be found hanging around outside PVR on a Saturday morning. It was an extraordinarily high number. I waited nervously, alone, for one of them to approach me. Thankfully none of them did – none of them looked at all like the kind of guy I'd like to have approached me for a blind date. (Looking back, I'm puzzled about what my parents were *thinking*, allowing me to go off to PVR on a blind date like that. No doubt I was quite confident and blasé when I told them about it, but honestly, how could they let me go off *alone* to meet a guy I'd never met before – outside PVR of all places? I'm sure I'll never let either of my daughters do any such thing, however grown-up they might be.)

After watching the green shirts for a while, I realized

that while many of them seemed to drift off with other people to be replaced by a fresh set of green shirts, there was one particular, glossy, dark green shirt that had been hanging around for a while now. I kept my eye on him and he avoided my eye. Ah. This must then be Vyom. I walked up to him, and even before I could say anything, we both knew we'd found each other. From that point on, there was no looking back.

When Amit and I had been neighbours, it had been a common friend who'd had to tell me that Amit was 'ding-dong' (what a way of putting it, even back in 1989!) over me. By then, we'd been neighbours for over a year, without saying more than an aloof 'hi' to each other.

Now that Amit had been in college for four years, and working in Bangalore for another year or so after that, it took Vyom to convey to me that Amit was, and had been all along (well, almost all along) still interested in me. It had not been Amit's intention – in either case – to convey this message through third parties; it was more that his interest in me was so clear to his friends that they just took it upon themselves to put him out of his misery by speaking to me on his behalf. It was probably a good idea – I don't think he could ever have done such a good job of it himself.

Ever since then, Vyom had been a dear friend, someone I genuinely liked and whose friendship I valued a great deal. So much so that I almost lost my job attempting to get leave to attend his wedding in Kolkata years later. (In the end, I got the leave *and* kept the job ... only to throw it away a few months later.)

Amit and I came to know Sridhar soon after we got married. He was, in their bachelor days, Vyom's colleague and flat-mate. One of the first few social outings that I had with Amit's friends after marriage was when we went to Vyom and Sridhar's bachelor pad one evening and Sridhar made matar-mushroom for us by following a recipe from a Sanjeev Kapoor book. It was delicious and I was hugely impressed. Sadly, he rarely repeated this foray into the culinary art for our benefit, but first impressions have extraordinary longevity, and I still have fond memories of that evening with matar-mushroom.

Over the years, after everyone was married and sundry other friends fell by the wayside or disappeared in the distance, the six of us became a gang. It was good to have a gang.

III

Since Amit and I were the first of the gang to get married, we were always expected to be the first to start a family. We knew that Vyom and Vipra would open their account soon. Sridhar and Sowmya were still discussing the matter, sometimes openly.

'What's the hurry?' asked Sridhar. 'We can have a baby after some years. I'm not ready right now. I have so many things to accomplish at work. There's an opportunity for us to go abroad for some time soon, let's wait for that to come through.'

'He'll never be ready,' said Sowmya, dismissively. 'And I don't know when that opportunity to go abroad will actually come. And I can't get a job because I'm always waiting to know when or if we're going to go abroad. Either we should go abroad now, or we should have a baby now. This way, I'm just unsettled.'

I listened to their arguments and thought back to when Amit and I had had so many of these. Sridhar never said never, but maybe Sowmya was right, maybe prevaricating was just his way of saying never. Maybe he never would be 'ready'. I had heard of so many men who hated to shoulder the responsibility of starting a family ... maybe all the wise old women were right – you should just go ahead and get pregnant anyway, and when the baby comes, the proud papa will be over the moon with delight.

It was one casual evening in February 2006 when the six of us had met for a prolonged coffee and gossip session at Java City, that Vyom quietly announced that Vipra was pregnant.

By this time, I was already beginning the long battle with depression and a sense of shame at our inability to conceive, and I hadn't really spoken to any of our friends about our situation. So I smiled happily and congratulated them warmly while, inside me, something tiny shattered into a million sharp pieces.

Now I'd have to watch these, our closest friends, go through several months of pregnancy, and I'd have to share their joy and their excitement and happy anticipation, and I'd have to be there at their side when the baby came. While we went on waiting, hoping, trying ... and getting nowhere.

It must have been a few months later when Arvind and Priya, also good friends of ours, though we didn't really meet them that often, shocked me by one day sending an SMS saying they'd had a baby girl. *Had!* I hadn't even known Priya was pregnant! I SMSed congratulations and mentally scratched them off my social list altogether. I didn't need yet another newborn in my social circle, reminding me so relentlessly of what I seemed to be incapable of having. It took many, many months of silence before I felt able to call Priya and explain our situation and why I'd been avoiding her.

There was yet another traumatic episode in store for me. Arvind and Soma were friends of Amit's from work. I knew them slightly, not very well. The fact that Soma was expecting a baby was only another nail in my bed of nails. It wasn't that information in itself that was difficult to bear – it was having to visit them in the maternity ward and congratulate them, smile delightedly and coo over the baby that – yet again – wasn't mine. If I couldn't be in

Soma's position, I would have given anything not to have to be there. If they had been my friends, I would have just explained honestly that I couldn't face it. But they were Amit's friends and at the time they knew nothing of our problems. So I went there and smiled, and came back home and cried.

In July that year, Vyom and Vipra's son was born. It was, conveniently, a Sunday. We went to the maternity home, together with Sridhar and Sowmya. Vipra looked exhausted, Vyom happy. The baby was just a baby, a bundle of cloth, a tiny, pink face, minute hands, invisible fingernails. Everyone took photos and videos, and I really tried to be happy for them, but my heart just wasn't in it. I caught Amit's eye.

'Don't worry,' he whispered to me, 'it'll be our turn next.'

But I knew that he couldn't possibly know that.

I was forced to face the inevitable: I would *have* to make another visit to the gynaecologist. And this time, I couldn't let myself be dismissed with stern admonitions to try harder and come back in two years.

TWO

Infertility

I

I went to Vipra's gynae. She was a nice doctor – patient, kind, polite.

'You've been trying to conceive for two years?' she asked me. 'Why did you wait so long? You should have consulted a doctor much earlier – given your age.'

She said it nicely, so I gritted my teeth and said nothing. She looked at my medical history and found that, at some point, I'd been diagnosed with polycystic ovary syndrome (PCOS). I had polycystic ovaries. I wasn't even aware of this. The diagnosis, made many years earlier, had never been explained to me. The doctor at that time had only advised me to continue with oral contraceptives. So I'd been on oral contraceptives for almost the whole time we'd been married – more than six years now.

'Let's first see if you are ovulating,' said Vipra's gynae cheerfully. 'If you have PCOS, you might not even be ovulating at all.'

I was devastated. Not even ovulating? All those months of trying – for nothing? 'Not even ovulating' made me sound completely defective – like an ATM machine that has no notes. Something you kick at, curse and move on to the next one.

'I can give you something to make you ovulate,' she said, 'or we can just wait and see.'

I elected to wait and see, and was scheduled for a series of scans in my next cycle, to check how my ovaries were doing. It turned out they were doing fine. If I had ever had PCOS, there was no sign of it now. On one of my follow-up visits, with my ovaries nicely enlarged as they should be, she gave me an injection to induce ovulation, and told me to go home and have sex. (She even dignified it by using its name, instead of using some terrible euphemism.)

That weekend, I was almost walking on air. My ovaries were fine. I was ovulating. I knew I was, because I'd had the shot and I could feel the pain. Now that I knew I was ovulating, if we had plenty of sex – and we did – surely I would conceive. Surely nothing could go wrong now?

We had planned a trip to Kolkata that October, and

off we duly went. All the time that we were there, I was hugging to myself the hope – the knowledge, it felt like – that I must be pregnant by now. It just *had* to have worked this time. I was *so* sure of it.

People asked me, 'Aren't you missing somebody in your life?' They said, 'Next time you come, bring a baby in your arms.' I smiled and nodded – I certainly hoped we would.

We were still in Kolkata when, bang on time, I got my period. It announced its arrival, as usual, with the tiniest smear of red on the toilet paper. I stared at it unbelievingly. Did I have piles? Maybe it was just spotting. Perhaps I ate something bright red in colour, like beetroot (which I hate). Anyway, it wasn't *menstrual* blood, it *couldn't* be. Whatever it was, it would go away.

But, of course, it didn't go away. A couple of days later, there was no denying that it was menstrual blood, and it wasn't just spotting.

There are no words to describe how I felt. Devastated, depressed, wretched, anguished, torn, useless ... none of these words can convey a fraction of what I felt. We were driving somewhere and I saw a cow that was obviously pregnant, and I thought, 'Even that stupid, brainless, grass-eating bovine can get pregnant, only I can't. I'm useless. I'm not worth anything at all. What good is my money, my education, my intelligence? I'm not even a fully functional woman.'

Yet, I could not show the slightest trace of my true emotions to the people around me. We were still in Kolkata, surrounded by Amit's extended family – warm, smiling, caring and cheerfully enquiring: when are you going to give us some 'good news'?

With Vipra's gynae, and with regular ultrasound scans to check for ovulation, we tried for another couple of months to conceive. When nothing worked, the doctor herself recommended that I visit a fertility clinic. 'You should have a hysterosalpingogram, HSG. There are options, but you need to go to a fertility clinic. There's nothing more I can do for you,' she said.

'But come back to me when you're pregnant.'

II

I showed no interest in finding a fertility clinic, so Amit asked around and set up an appointment. We reached on the given day at the given time (a weekday morning), and were made to wait for well over an hour. The gynaecologist's husband had a paediatric clinic at the same premises, so the entire time we waited, a parade of newborns and infants went past us, proud mothers beaming while I sank deeper and deeper in shame at my failure.

At last the doctor came, and we were summoned.

'How long have you been married?'

'About eight years.'

'And how long have you been trying to conceive?'

'Only the last two years. Before that I was using the oral contraceptive.'

'For how long?'

'For about six years.'

'And now you have been trying to conceive for only two years. That's the problem with all you young people nowadays. You waste so many years using all kinds of contraceptives and then you think that when you want to get pregnant, it should happen right away.'

I was shocked speechless. Was this doctor *blaming me* for not being able to get pregnant? Was she judging me for not having had babies already? It wasn't even my fault! I glanced at Amit, waiting for him to say that it was he who had made us wait. But he was impassive, he hadn't noticed anything amiss.

'Do you experience any discomfort during intercourse? Or when passing urine?' asked the doctor.

I shook my head mutely.

'None?' she asked impatiently.

'No,' I said, still close to tears.

'Well, you've probably got a urine infection anyway. Have you done your hormone tests?'

I had – Vipra's gynaecologist had made me and Amit get our tests done, as a matter of routine. My thyroid stimulating hormone (TSH) and prolactin levels had been tested. Everything appeared normal. I handed over the report.

'TSH normal? Prolactin normal? Hmmm... Well, you've probably got a hormone imbalance as well. Probably you're not ovulating.'

I explained that my periods were regular, and that I'd done a series of scans over the past few months that showed I was ovulating normally.

'Okay, let me do an internal exam,' she said.

I wasn't sure she'd even heard me.

It was the most hateful internal exam I'd ever had – probably because I hated the doctor by now, and I felt humiliated by the whole process, right from the waiting outside while beaming mothers with healthy babies paraded past me to having my legs strung up while she peered and poked in my private parts.

In the end, she prescribed: Doxycycline, an antibiotic, against a possible (but, in my opinion, imaginary) urinary tract infection; Secnil Forte for vaginitis (which I had no evidence of either); a Clotrimazole pessary (yes, a pessary! You have to insert it!) called Cansoft, an antifungal (just-in-case); and finally Siphene (Clomiphene Citrate, also known as Clomid) to make me ovulate.

'Start on Siphene after you've completed the other medications. Try it for six months. Come in for the ultrasound scans three or four times each month, and when it shows that you're ovulating, have intercourse.'

'And what if...'

'If that doesn't work, we'll do the HSG and after that we'll try a laparoscopy. All of this will take about a year, after that we'll go on to intrauterine insemination (IUI) and in vitro fertilization (IVF). After all, you've waited so long, you can wait a little longer, can't you?'

'But...'

'Don't worry, I've delivered babies even when the mother was thirty-nine,' she said with an evil smile as she waited for us to leave.

I walked out of her clinic in tears. I didn't *want* to have a baby when I was thirty-nine. I wanted to have *two* babies, and I wanted them before I was *thirty-five*. Of course, that looked impossible already and I didn't need a doctor to tell me that. But I also didn't need a doctor to lecture me, pass judgement on me, or call me wicked for not wanting to have babies as soon as I possibly could. I wanted a doctor who would just do her work – find out what was wrong with me, and fix it if it could be fixed. And I didn't see any evidence that this doctor even knew what she was doing. She'd just loaded me with medicines without any apparent justification. I was no doctor, but I had some sense and I had the Internet. Most of the websites didn't even recommend trying more than three months with Clomid. And besides, Clomid only worked on women who *weren't* ovulating; it didn't work if there was some other cause behind your inability to conceive. Of course –

that's what all the other drugs were for. Why bother with procedure and diagnosis and all that rigmarole? If you throw the pharmacy at a person, *something* should work.

'I'm never going back there again,' was the first thing I said to Amit.

'Why?' he asked.

I stared at him, dumbstruck.

'Of course, I realized you didn't like her. Was there something in particular, or was it just an ego thing?' he asked.

'What ego thing?' I asked.

'Well, your ego thing – you know, where you don't like women who are more assertive than you are.'

My 'ego thing'? Wait, wasn't this guy supposed to be on *my* side? I tried to explain to him what had just happened and why I felt upset about it, but he didn't get it, so in the end I gave up and retired to lick my wounds alone.

III

So traumatic was this experience for me, that many months passed before I was even willing to consider any kind of doctor again. I took the medicines she gave me, but of course nothing worked. The Clomid gave me severe ovulation pain, but nothing more exciting than that.

I continued to go for the ultrasound scans regularly every month. I hated them, though. The first ultrasound I'd had had been so easy, quick and painless that I'd been thoroughly relieved. All you had to do was to drink a litre of water and wait. Then, once the water had made it to your bladder and it was nicely full, you were told to lie down for a couple of minutes. They squirted something on your tummy area – a little lower, but still on a decent part of your anatomy – and rolled what looked a bit like a computer mouse over you. And that was it. You got up and rushed to the toilet.

So, apart from having to suffer a somewhat tight bladder for a bit, the ultrasounds initially were not too bad.

Then, a couple of times, I was made to wait for the technician. Waiting for half an hour with a full bladder is bad. Really, really bad. So bad, that the second time I vented my frustration on the technician in no uncertain terms.

'Don't worry, madam,' she replied patiently and sweetly, 'next time I'll do an internal scan.'

At once, my fury evaporated. What! An internal scan? Ugh. That wasn't what I wanted at all! 'No, no, it's okay, only don't keep me waiting for twenty-five minutes, that's all,' I said in a placatory tone. Mentally, I made a note to drink a little less water next time. But it was to no avail. As soon as she saw me the next time, the sweet young girl told me to go to the toilet because she didn't need a full bladder, she needed it empty. She was going to do an internal scan.

Meekly, I did as instructed and returned to lie on the bed, naked below the waist. It is completely humiliating to have to lie on a hospital bed, naked below the waist, while strange doctors stick strange things in between your legs. I was partly shocked and partly relieved when I saw her open a condom and slip it on to the probe: at least the condom was a known object. Still, it was altogether pretty awful.

I went for two or three scans each month, and they all showed I was ovulating, but every time, two weeks later, there would be the familiar and hateful signs of my failure, yet again, to conceive.

Through all of this, life went on. I continued to work, continued to meet people, continued my hobbies and interests. Though it was increasingly difficult to appear 'normal' and cheerful, I confided in very few people – I didn't find it easy to talk about this, and I don't think most people found it easy to respond. Too often, when I did broach the subject, I got (well-meant but) stupid platitudes in response:

'Just relax, it will happen when you least expect it.'

'Take a holiday.'

'It's all because of too much stress. Why don't you quit your job and stay home for a while?'

'You should play with other people's babies, it gets the hormones going.'

'Well, you can always adopt.'

These were at best infuriating, at worst completely

insensitive. Play with other people's babies? What, so I can realize afresh what it is that I'm missing and how much it hurts? Relax? *You* try to relax when you're thirty-three and haven't been able to get pregnant for the last three years. When I least expect it? Then it'll probably happen when I'm fifty-five, because right now, I don't think there's going to be any least expecting it. As for adopting: *Do you think that's really what I want to hear when what I'm trying for is to get pregnant?*

Maybe any answer is the wrong answer in this situation. Perhaps there is no right answer at all. Perhaps the best reply is just silence, or non-verbal sympathy. Every problem does not have a solution, so these trite replies just don't work. At least they didn't work for me.

THREE

The End of the Road

I

Time dragged on, and I continued to struggle with depression. There were a lot of jumbled emotions: shame, frustration, a sense of being a failure, and that completely pointless question, 'why me?' – but most of all, there was depression.

All the visits to the doctors, all the tests, internal exams, the invasiveness, the humiliation of opening your body and your sex life up for examination by total strangers, and the ultimate futility of all those things had taken it out of me. At first, I used to hope that everything was okay with both of us; but later I began to wish desperately that something *was* wrong, and that with the next test, the next appointment, they would find out just what it was and how to fix it.

The not-knowing, the suspense, was perhaps the most unbearable part of the whole affair. I felt, at times, that I wouldn't even have minded knowing the worst, just as long as I could get past it and get on with life. Being stuck in the 'trying' phase – with all its monthly cycle of hope and despair – was just unbearable.

Amit was not as emotionally invested, nor was he very understanding of my involvement. He had other thoughts to keep him occupied. For me, by then, this was the one overriding thought, always occupying the top two-thirds of my mind. I woke up wondering when it would ever happen, and I fell asleep with that question preying on my mind. Was this obsession? Was it possible to be in this position and not be obsessed? If having a baby wasn't necessarily the biggest thing in a person's life, not having one when you wanted it, desperately, certainly was.

I turned to the Internet for information and solace and soon found that the two were mutually exclusive. Information there was – but much of it was even more depressing than my former ignorance:

- About one in six or seven couples face infertility.
- Even couples who have already had one or more babies can become infertile – it is called secondary infertility.
- Male factor infertility is – in many studies – as commonly

the cause for infertility as female factor.

- According to some estimates, in as many as 20 to 30 per cent of cases, both partners have issues resulting in infertility.
- It is not always possible to identify the reason for a couple's infertility. From 10 to 25 per cent of infertility cases remain unexplained.
- The longer you've been trying without success to conceive, the less likely is it to happen naturally.
- A 30 per cent or higher success rate for IVF is considered good. (That's *good*!)
- You can't try IVF three or four times and expect the odds to work out for you – no matter how many times you try, your chance of success on any particular attempt is still only about 30 per cent.

Solace was hard to find. I read of other couples struggling with fertility issues, and they reduced me to tears. Successes, failures, and ongoing ordeals – nothing seemed to offer any real hope for me. Many of the treatments seemed horrific: invasive, mechanical, time-consuming and incredibly expensive.

I read as much as I could about causes, diagnostic procedures and possible outcomes. The facts were often difficult to digest, the figures impossible.

I tried to imagine going through IVF – Amit goes alone into a room to watch a dirty movie and provide the 'sample'. I go into another room where doctors extract my eggs. The two are mixed in a glass container with doctors and technicians squinting at them to ensure that they mix properly. Then, if egg and sperm have done what they are supposed to do, more doctors and syringes squirting the 'live' embryos directly into my uterus. I had always thought of conception as a possible outcome of sex – a natural and straightforward process. This laboratory-oriented process just seemed so unnatural, so wrong. There would be half a dozen doctors and technicians involved, strangers, people interested only in the science of reproduction. Sex had never seemed as impersonal, repulsive and unnatural as this sounded.

Then I read about how, with IVF, it was possible that multiple embryos would be formed and some would be put into my womb and allowed to become babies, while others would be kept frozen and eventually, presumably, just abandoned to their fate. Worse, if multiple embryos were implanted in the womb, sometimes a few were later removed to give the others a better chance of survival. All those embryos that were so casually disposed of, could actually have gone on to become my babies.

All of this seemed unimaginable to me. Could I, so cavalierly, play god with so many potential babies of ours, killing some, freezing some, and allowing others to grow and be born? Science said they were only embryos, only a random collection of cells, but my emotions and instincts wouldn't allow me to see them as anything other than future children of mine.

So, at various levels, IVF and related procedures did not seem like much of an option to me. Apart from the emotional aspect, they would also, clearly, be a huge drain on our financial resources.

By this time, I was very familiar with the endless cycle of hope and despair, of pathetic yearning and praying followed by sheer anguish and hopelessness, that every new month brought. If we did a couple of attempts at IUI and another three or four attempts at IVF, we'd spend close to another year in this endless cycle of hope and despair. It was tearing me apart, and I wasn't sure how much longer I could go on like that. A small part of me just wanted it to end – if we couldn't have kids, we couldn't have kids; and much though I'd fought with Amit *to* have kids, now I'd just have to accept that it was never meant to be. If Nature herself was against you, there really was no point in going on trying.

Just as I was beginning to think that I wanted to step off this merry-go-round, my parents came to visit for a few days. Naturally, this subject came up for discussion. And, at some point, although all I wanted was to flee from the scene, lock myself in a room and throw away the key, somehow I agreed to see another doctor.

II

I had another brief and mildly discouraging experience with yet another doctor who kept me waiting for a long time and finally never turned up for the appointment. After all I'd been through already, this was only a minor irritant, but I wasn't in the frame of mind to tolerate even minor irritants. So, for our next attempt, Amit got us an appointment at Manipal Hospital, a large and well-reputed hospital in Bangalore.

At the hospital, our department was called ART. I thought it a funny name for an infertility clinic, till I found out that it stood for Assisted Reproduction Technique or some such thing. It was on the ninth floor – nowhere near the obstetrics and gynaecology or paediatric departments, which was a relief. In the waiting room, we sat amidst other couples looking equally anxious, depressed and eager to avoid our eyes.

Of all places in the world that I can think of where I *wouldn't* want to meet someone I know, this has got to rate among the top ten. Or maybe the top two. In a gynaecologist's clinic, there could be any number of reasons to be waiting; but in an infertility clinic, there's only one – and it's not one you want to talk to anyone about, least of all to people you might have met in a formal setting. I met a couple I'd known in a German-language course I'd taken. While we exchanged polite, embarrassed hellos, the husband was called in to the 'sample room'.

Uh-oh – I don't even want to think about that.

We were called punctually. Our doctor – my doctor, actually; there was a separate doctor for men – was female (of course) and quite old. She was neither sympathetic nor judgemental, merely professional and matter-of-fact. She was also the first doctor with whom I didn't feel rushed or under any pressure. I asked her questions based on what I'd read on the Internet, and she didn't seem threatened by it. She answered reasonably and calmly.

'I've taken the Clomid for three months already,' I told her, as soon as I'd given her most of my case history. 'Should I continue it in the next cycle?' I was praying she'd say no.

She looked at various reports I'd handed to her. 'I don't see any evidence that we need to stimulate ovulation for you,' she said thoughtfully. 'You seem to be ovulating without it. I think you can stop it for now.'

If that made me think well of her, what followed almost deified her in my esteem. First, she refused to start any course of treatment or medication for me without further tests. 'There's no point in my just loading you with hormones until we know what the problem is,' she said. 'Let's check your hormone levels first, and we'll also do an HSG if required.'

HSG. I didn't even like the sound of it.

'It's a simple procedure. You'll just have to take one day off from work,' she added, noticing my apprehension. 'It'll be mildly uncomfortable, but not painful. It's mainly diagnostic, just to see if there's anything wrong.' If she had said it any other way, I would have rejected the suggestion outright, but because she was so reassuring about it, and because she didn't try to pressure me in any way, I thought I might try it – if I absolutely had to. It was, as she said, mainly diagnostic. If they could find a problem, it would put me out of my misery; if they could fix it, even better. At any rate, it wasn't, in itself, aided conception. The conception would happen, if it did, the normal way.

But first, there were more tests to be done. I had to do pretty much a complete blood test, along with blood sugar tests (glucose and insulin), more hormone tests (folicle-stimulating hormone, FSH, and lutenizing hormone, LH), and a urine test. For some of those, I'd have to come back at the appropriate time in my cycle.

She also suggested that Amit get himself tested again. He had to do a whole host of hormone tests too, as well as a semen analysis.

'I've already done that,' he pointed out, indicating the report.

'It's better if you do the tests again, at the lab here,' she said mildly.

At last, we got up to go. 'Don't you want to examine her?' asked Amit.

I could have killed him right then, but the doctor shook her head.

'There's nothing more that an exam can tell me right now,' she said. 'Let me see those test reports first.'

That was such a relief. In those days, anyone who *didn't* want me to spreadeagle myself on a hospital bed so they could do vulgar things to me was way up there in my list of people I didn't mind meeting.

With this doctor, I felt cautiously optimistic. She seemed to know what she was doing; her approach was completely in line with whatever I'd read on the Internet. She was patient and calm and answered all my questions systematically. She didn't seem to mind having a 'participatory' patient. At last, I thought, I'd found a doctor I could cope with.

III

Now that we seemed to be going about things the right away, I felt resigned to waiting and hoping – hoping to find out soon what was wrong.

It wasn't as much of a wait as we'd been expecting. One week later, we had the answer. My blood test results were all normal. So were Amit's. But the semen analysis showed there was a serious problem with sperm motility. Most (85 per cent) of the sperm just weren't swimming. Technically, it was called severe asthenospermia.

'With these figures, the chances of your ever conceiving naturally is practically zero,' said the technician candidly, while handing Amit the test result. I can't imagine how he felt at that moment, but I can only be sure that it was nothing like how I would have felt in his position.

Why hadn't the earlier test caught it?

'The other lab probably did a "sink test",' said my mother when we brought her up to date. 'They must have thrown the sample down the sink and written up a random report within the normal parameters.'

It was an unpleasant thought, but seemed like the most probable explanation of the widely differing reports. This didn't seem to be a condition that changed markedly over a period of weeks or months. Or ever, in fact.

So now we knew.

We were shattered ... but also relieved. Now, at last, we could stop wondering *whether* anything was wrong, and if so, *what*. At last, I could begin to shake off the feeling of being 'defective'. If Amit ever felt that way, it was something he dealt with much more effectively and much less visibly than I had done. He seemed to shrug it off as something he had no control over.

That day, after about half an hour spent on the Net, we knew that we had reached the end of the road. The condition could not be treated – sperm either swam, or didn't; there was no way to coax them to swim. There were some means of finding the root cause of the condition, but this didn't help in arriving at any cure, so it was of largely academic interest. We continued to search for information for a couple of hours, but the first half hour said it all – this was the end of the road for us.

Assisted conception in such cases involved a specialized form of IVF, IVF with ICSI (intracytoplasmic sperm injection), which involved isolating a single sperm cell and deliberately injecting it right into the egg that had been recovered from the woman. It was interesting to read about in an academic, impersonal way, but I didn't want any baby of mine being born that way. It was as 'artificial' as regular IVF, but with some added complications and risks. In this process too multiple embryos would be created and some of them would later be discarded.

There were other considerations too. IVF with ICSI was more technically challenging than regular IVF, which meant that success rates were lower and costs were higher. The success rate worried me. I hadn't coped particularly well so far with all the suspense of trying to conceive. I wasn't at all sure that I could go through many more months of the agonizing ups and downs. Besides, we didn't know whether there was some as-yet-undiscovered problem in me, which would further influence the success rate of IVF. If we did want to consider IVF, I would have to go through a further battery of tests and examinations and scans and whatnot to verify that. And it would require a significant investment of time and energy – it didn't sound like something you could do over a weekend or by taking a day off every so often.

In any case, IVF had never been a very appealing option for either of us, and with the latest information, we decided to scratch it off our list of options altogether.

That simplified things. Now I could finally step off the merry-go-round of hope and despair. We now had only two options to consider: to remain childless for life, or to adopt.

FOUR

Deciding to Adopt

I

In a way, life had come full circle, back to the point when, a few years ago, I tried desperately to tell myself that it *wasn't* all that important to have a child (or two), that life *could* be fulfilling and fun without them.

It's not that I had always wanted to have kids. When I was younger, for the longest time I quite firmly *didn't* want to have kids. I thought they were an encumbrance. Whiny. Demanding. Irritating.

Some years later, I still didn't want to have kids, but by then I thought that I *might* – some day – want to, and that it might perhaps be something I *should* do. It was an integral part of life, wasn't it? An experience that I'd want to have, want to cherish?

At that point, I still didn't think kids were cute. That came later.

I don't actually know when or how the change came about, but gradually I started thinking more about raising kids, about things I would do and wouldn't do with my kids, then about actually having kids. I started noticing babies and toddlers. Then, I started dreaming of having babies of my own. And finally I was planning it. I was thinking of names, planning baby furniture, even deciding whether I'd want to have the delivery in Bangalore, or back where my parents were, the city I grew up in – Chandigarh.

That had been years ago. After that followed all the trouble with Amit. And after that battle, this.

Was it time to accept that this was something that was never meant to be? Maybe I should just accept that, for whatever reason, fate, god or whatever runs this mysterious universe had decided that I, Anamika, would be one of the chosen few who would never raise a family? Never pass on her genes? Never have a pair of innocent baby eyes looking into hers with complete, unquestioning trust and devotion? Dog eyes, maybe – I could still get a dog some day – but not baby eyes. Devout dog lover though I am, I could still tell there was a difference.

It was a bitter pill to swallow, just as bitter (or more so) the second time round. It was strange to think that, fifteen years ago, if somebody had told me I'd some day want desperately to have kids, I'd only have given them a highly sceptical look. When and how did I get from over there to over here?

By this time, most of our family and close friends knew that we were having trouble conceiving. There didn't seem any point in keeping quiet about it now – nothing was going to change. In fact, I found that it was easier for me to tell people whom I hadn't been able to talk to before. I didn't have to say, 'I don't know.' I didn't have to say, 'Maybe never.'

I just said, 'Never, actually.'

Sometimes, if I didn't particularly like the person or the way they had asked the question, I added coldly, 'We can't.' That embarrassed most people into silence.

In between the sympathy and the awkward silences, lots of people said, 'Well, you can always adopt.'

II

It was still a very difficult time for me, especially whenever I met people who had children – which was often. Vyom and Vipra's son, Vidit, was several months old by this time. We had met them a few times. Each time was difficult, but at last it became almost unbearable for me. I couldn't bear looking at their warm, gushing happiness. Vyom's relaxed, cheerful face as he played with Vidit; Vipra tired, fond, scolding, indulgent. When, oh when, would we ever get there, I used to think. Overnight, I had been forced to accept that we never would.

'I can't bear to meet them any more,' I told Amit one day, after a particularly cruel evening out with them.

'But they are our friends,' he protested gently. He found it difficult too, I knew that. 'How can we avoid meeting them?'

'We could just tell them,' I said. 'I'm sure they'd understand.'

But Amit didn't think it was a good idea. 'They'll feel hurt,' he said. 'They want us to share their joy.'

One day when I was chatting with Vyom on instant messenger, I told him. Vyom is a sensible and sensitive person. I don't know if he understood, but he did understand that whatever I said, there was no malice, no ill will of any kind, hardly even any jealousy ... and he wasn't upset. 'You'll get over it gradually,' he said. 'You can come over and play with Vidit any time, maybe it'll help you feel better.'

It wasn't the most sensible suggestion to make to me at that point, but I knew he was only trying to help. 'It makes me feel wretched,' I said.

'Okay, then come when you want to. Amit can come on his own, if he feels like it.'

I left it at that; Amit could explain his part himself, if he wanted to.

I spoke to Priya, finally, too. She was very understanding.

'I know another couple who've recently gone through this,' she said. It made me feel even more miserable for not confiding in her earlier. I continued to avoid her for a while.

We suddenly seemed to have very few friends who didn't already have kids. Sridhar and Sowmya were still, mercifully, at odds with each other about it; and another couple of close friends of mine were recently married but not in the family way yet. These few friends became the bulwarks of my social life. But I lived in perpetual dread of hearing the 'good news' from any of them – I could not imagine avoiding them, but I also couldn't face the thought of yet another close friend getting pregnant and having a baby while I looked on and tried to feel happy.

For several months, I didn't want to think about adoption. I didn't want to reopen the painful thought or the yearning to have kids. I just wanted to get on with my life – to push the whole sordid affair aside and pick up the widely scattered pieces of my life. I let the disappointment of 'never' settle deep in my heart and mind.

Over the months, there came a sort of peace, a kind of acceptance. At least I was no longer dreading my period. I still had a faint, faint hope that it might not come, but there was none of the anguish when it did. In fact, that tiny, almost unnoticeable flicker of hope remained with me for years. Even now, sometimes, I feel its feeble presence. Perhaps it will remain forever, until my periods themselves go away and take with them every last possibility of my ever being pregnant.

III

After some months, the idea of adoption began to play around in the back of my mind. I can't say that I took to it immediately. It was hard to accept that I would have to settle for a child that wasn't really 'mine'. It wouldn't look like us, it wouldn't have our genes. It would be somebody else's child. Could I really love such a child? Would I worry about where it came from and how it came to be? What if it were a prostitute's child?

Why did this worry me? On the face of it, I was worried about the baby's health – how much care would a prostitute be able to take of her health while she was pregnant? But there was something more to it, something less definable. I think I wanted to think of my baby as being conceived out of love ... or at least, not out of an indifferent and unspecified commercial lust, and especially not out of a violent and vicious rape. Yes, such things worried me – a little.

Luckily, there were other things I didn't worry about. I didn't care what time of day, month, or year the child was born, and under what star. I didn't worry about the caste, community, or religion of the child's parents. Very soon, I stopped worrying about their morals and professions as well. A child, I decided, if not entirely a *tabula rasa* – a blank state – was at least largely so. If we took a child in, it would surely adopt our culture and beliefs. The younger it were, the easier it would be. Even if it were the illegal offspring of a prostitute and a murderer, those characteristics would not be in its genes. And I for one, I decided firmly, would not want to hold against a baby the sins of its parents.

But would I be able to love the child? This was my greatest fear. I had never been pregnant, but I had some fairy-tale notion that you began to love the child growing inside you long before you ever saw it. That bond, I felt, began as soon as you knew you were pregnant, and only grew stronger after the baby was born. I know that there are plenty of biological mothers out there who can tell me in how many ways I am wrong about this, but this was my conviction. Take away the pregnancy and labour and delivery, and what do you have left?

On the other hand, I had grown up with dogs and I had loved them with every little bit of my heart. They were neither my biological children, nor my biological siblings – they were adopted, as all pets are – but that didn't stop me from loving them completely. Why should it be less so with a baby?

Because, my brain reminded me remorselessly, dogs are not babies and babies are not dogs.

As before, I turned to the Internet. All that I read on the Internet indicated that everyone who had ever felt this way before adopting always had only good things to say once they had actually adopted a baby. Yes, I read time and again, you can and do love an adopted child as much as a biological child. Even parents who had had children both ways agreed that there was no difference in the way you love your child.

When I was still not quite convinced, I broached the subject with Amit. To my surprise and delight, he was open to the idea.

'You won't know whose baby it is,' I warned him. 'It could be a prostitute's baby.'

'That doesn't matter,' he said at once. 'As long as it is healthy, how does it matter?'

The moment he said it, I knew that it really didn't matter to me either.

'It won't look like us,' I went on.

'Yes, but if we had a child with your brains and my looks, that wouldn't have been a recipe for success either,' he dead-panned.

'Yes, but just think – if it had had my brains and *my* looks …' I retorted.

'Then it's probably better that we adopt.'

'But won't it be strange, bringing someone else's baby into our house?' I asked when we had stopped laughing.

'Yes, maybe, a little. But I'm sure we'll grow to love him

or her soon,' said Amit, reassuringly.

Though I had been the one to bring up adoption, he seemed to have far fewer doubts than me.

'We only have to make sure the baby is totally healthy,' he said. 'We don't know how much care the mother would have taken during pregnancy, so we must make sure that there are no congenital defects and that development is normal as far as possible.'

In fact, long after all my doubts and fears had disappeared, long after our girls became an inextricable part of our family, I continued to think about the genetic aspect of adoption. The nature versus nurture discussion raises the fundamental issue – do genes determine a person, or does the environment? Obviously both play a role, but which is greater, which is the overriding determinant of a person's character, their health and, therefore, to some extent their future? The more medical science progresses, the more it appears that genetics determines everything: from the colour of your eyes, skin and hair, to your likelihood of developing diabetes, heart disease, or schizophrenia. Some studies even show that criminality and alcoholism tend to run in families – to say nothing of psychosocial disorders, intelligence, creative abilities and whatnot.

But the more I think of it, the more I realize that this too is a spurious argument against adoption. Our genetic make-up certainly plays a role in determining our health and personality, but there is still no guarantee that the biological child of two healthy parents will be healthy. There is not even any guarantee that, of two identical twins, both will be equally healthy. There are sufficient instances of identical twins who suffer from different supposedly genetic conditions to show that genes do not bear the sole responsibility for how we turn out. Ultimately, the thought that our genes are better that somebody else's is inherently not only fallacious, but also ethically and morally wrong. A child who is genetically ours is starting out with as clean or as murky a slate as a child who isn't – this is what I have come to believe.

In all our discussions, the only mild, hardly spoken regret I heard from Amit was that a child who was not biologically ours would not inherit his extra-tall genes. Amit himself is seven feet tall, and many of his family members are quite tall, so there is a tall gene in his family. 'But of course, since you are only five-foot-nothing, our biological child might not have been very tall either,' he admitted stoically. And that, in a nutshell, was that.

IV

When we had largely agreed that we would adopt, I decided that I should speak to someone who had adopted, to get a better understanding of the process and to check that we weren't completely overlooking something on either the procedural or the emotional front. I hunted around for people I knew who had adopted. They weren't difficult to find. If you talk to people you know, you're sure to find someone who knows someone who has adopted. Despite being shy about talking to strangers on the phone – and on an intensely personal subject at that – I called up several people who had adopted.

'It was terrible,' said Arvind, a friend's friend in Mumbai. 'My wife and I had to go to Pune for the adoption. The agency called us about two weeks before and gave us a date. The day before we left, they told us that two babies were available and we could choose either one.'

'Oh, did you have to choose?' I asked in surprise. Most of the websites advocated against allowing (or making) parents choose, and it sounded pretty traumatic to me too.

'Yes, they said they had two babies and we could choose,' repeated Arvind. 'My wife was so nervous, she said she couldn't go, I should call them up and cancel the whole adoption process. But I told her, let's at least go and see, if we can't do it, we'll come back.

'When we got there, they straightaway took us to a room and showed us one baby girl. And that was it. We said yes right away. They asked us if we would like to see the other girl, we said no. Then we had to go to the hospital, get the tests done, and then we could go home. Within a few months all the paperwork was done and now she's almost one year old!'

It was such a daunting thing, but here was someone telling me it could be done. The others had similar stories, similar experiences; the details were different each time, but each story had a happy ending – happy parents and a happy baby.

By this time, Amit and I were convinced that we could script our own happy ending. As prospective adoptive parents, we were fairly easy-going in our requirements. In discussions with other people about adoption, many of whom had considered adoption and not gone through with it, some or all of the following had been advanced as criteria – or at least points for consideration – in the decision on whether or not to adopt (listed here in no particular order):

- Gender
- Age at the time of adoption
- Age at the time of being given up for adoption
- Looks and complexion
- General health – height, weight and overall development
- Diseases, disabilities, or congenital conditions, if any
- Date and time of birth or assumed date and time of birth; sun sign
- Marital status or nature of relationship between biological parents

- Reason for being given for adoption
- General health of biological parents – predisposition to genetic diseases or conditions
- Health of biological mother during pregnancy – exposure to / use of tobacco, alcohol, or other harmful or toxic substances
- Economic status of biological parents
- Caste of biological parents
- Religious affiliations of biological parents
- Moral and ethical values of biological parents
- Whether or not biological parents were vegetarians

Just about the only things I haven't heard mentioned were the political affiliations of the biological parents and whether they preferred tea or coffee.

I could understand that many of these could be very serious considerations for people, especially those with strong cultural or religious beliefs. For us, in many ways, once we got past the infertility, the decision to adopt was one that came easily, quickly and relatively painlessly; we were lucky that way.

Only one thing continued to hold me back. If we adopted a child, we would have our family at last; but it still wouldn't be *mine*. I wouldn't ever be pregnant; I wouldn't ever have my obstetrics-gynaecology-pregnancy-delivery room stories to share in discussions at the workplace; and I would never be able to point out with pride – or accept as a compliment – how my genes, or Amit's, showed in the child's looks, intelligence, or abilities.

I mourned for my unconceived child, for my impossible pregnancy. It took many months before that loss diminished to an almost unnoticeable level. But, even as I resigned myself to never being a biological mother, I took the first step towards being an adoptive mother.

FIVE

The Road to Adoption

I

In August 2006, just after Vidit was born to Vyom and Vipra, but just before I began to drown in our infertility woes, Amit and I went for a trek in Ladakh. This was not unusual; we had trekked several times, and had been to Ladakh a couple of times before. On 25 August, we had been back in Bangalore for a few days. We were still feeling good about our holiday, not yet swamped by the routine of everyday life. On that day, unknown to any of us, at 5.30 in the morning, some other woman gave birth to our children in a hospital in Pondicherry.

It was, from what little we know, a full-term pregnancy, and a normal delivery. The babies were healthy, and weighed in at about 2.75 kg each – normal for twins, and the lower end of normal for single babies.

As per the Indian adoption regulations, we know nothing about the twins' biological parents. We can only speculate about their situation and circumstances. What we do know is that, the day after their birth, their biological mother left the hospital, leaving her babies behind. I can only imagine what that must have been like for her. Some people tend to think that the mother must be completely heartless to leave her children, but I'm not sure it is as simple as that. There could be circumstances that compelled her to do so; I can think of several. Perhaps she already had children, and too few resources to raise two more. Perhaps she was under pressure to produce sons ('otherwise don't bother bringing them home'). Perhaps she had been recently widowed, or deserted by her husband. Perhaps she was too young, or unmarried. Perhaps she had no information about, or no access to, contraceptives. Perhaps she could not enforce the use of a condom by her partner. Perhaps she had been raped.

It is unfair to assume that she left her babies as she did, without a backward glance, without a second thought. We can't know just how she felt – before, at the time of, or months or years after the act – knowing she'd left her newborn babies out there, alone in a hostile world. Maybe she agonized over her decision. Maybe she still sometimes wonders what became of them. Maybe she regrets it.

Maybe she hopes that they found a loving family and a better life than she could provide.

Our babies were lucky – they were safe in the hospital. Within a day or two, they were safely in charge of the orphanage that would be their home for the next thirteen months. They were named Inmathy (later Mrinalinee, which we shortened to Mrini) and Illavarasi (Nayantara, called Tara). They did not, perhaps, have the healthiest and happiest infancy possible in the agency; their growth was below par and they were not exactly the picture of health when we saw them at thirteen months. But at least they were in a safe environment, where basic food, security and health care were assured.

Over a period of several months, their paperwork was processed. Babies who are abandoned cannot be put up for adoption right away. The law decrees that every effort be made to trace the biological parents, who can either claim the child, or sign documents waiving their rights as parents. The agency must check the given address, if they have one, and also place advertisements in the local newspapers. If, after all this, and after a suitable interval of time has passed, no biological parents can be found, then the agency can get a court order declaring the child free for adoption.

Next comes the task of finding a family for the child. When we went to claim our children, we were told that three prospective adoptive parents had been contacted for the twins before us. Strangely enough, nobody wanted twin girls – and so it came to our turn. But the entire process took time. Each family must be contacted, and given a chance to accept the child. After each of the three families had declined, the agency contacted the office of the central governing body in Tamil Nadu, the Adoption Coordinating Agency (ACA), which contacted the Karnataka ACA, and it in turn contacted us.

II

It was sometime late in the first half of 2007 when Amit and I took the first step towards adoption. We drove down to the Karnataka ACA early one Saturday morning. I had spent a good part of the week speaking to various adoption agencies in Bangalore on the phone. Each of them assured me that there was a long waiting period.

'If you want a boy it will take more than two years,' they all said.

'We're not particular. We can adopt a girl also,' I said. Actually, I liked the thought of a girl. Whenever I dreamt of having a family, I dreamt of having at least one daughter. Two daughters would have been fine too. If I had had children naturally, and if they had both (or all, if we had more than two) been boys, I don't know how I would have managed. Amit, in his usual contrarian fashion, decided he wanted a boy.

'Let's just apply and see what we get,' I said.

'That means we'll get a girl,' he said, prosaically.

The adoption agencies I spoke to confirmed this. Girls were always more easily available than boys.

'If getting a girl means waiting a year or more, and getting a boy means waiting for two years or more...' I said to Amit.

'We'll get a girl,' he conceded. He too was eager to just get our family started.

When I spoke to the ACA, they also said that the waiting period for boys would be about two years, and for girls, about a year or more. I'd spoken to or heard of several people by now who had already adopted girls – and none of them had had to wait for so long. About four or five months was what most people said. But none of them was based in Bangalore, so I thought that perhaps Karnataka was slower than other states. Maybe they were more thorough with the paperwork. Maybe there were fewer children put up for adoption. Maybe there were more couples looking to adopt.

The only practical way to adopt in India is to do so in the state in which you live. We had family in Delhi, Chandigarh and Kolkata, but if we tried to adopt from those places, or from any of our neighbouring states, it would only complicate the paperwork. So we resigned ourselves to just waiting it out.

'What's the difference between applying through an agency and applying to the ACA?' I asked the ACA representative over the phone.

'Well, if you apply to an agency, you will be on their waiting list. Any baby who is with them, who is free for adoption, can come to you. So it is a smaller set of babies, but also a smaller pool of parents. Each agency has to coordinate with us, and if they are unable to place a baby, they inform us. We don't have any babies for adoption directly with us. If you apply to us, we will coordinate with all the agencies and let you know as soon as any agency has a baby that they are unable to place. Also, if you are interested in adopting from any other state, we can co-ordinate that, but agencies can't do that.'

It seemed like a good enough reason to apply directly with the ACA, so I made an appointment with a social worker called Laveena.

The ACA office was far away, small and rather homey. There was a school attached to it, so we could see a lot of small kids coming and going as we waited (which wasn't long). Laveena turned out to be a large, pleasant, and cheerful woman. She spoke to us at length about our reasons for wanting to adopt, our family background, whether anyone in our family was against the adoption, whether we would talk to our adopted child about their adoption and so on. She walked us through the process too.

'First you should consider the decision for another month. Then you can come back and register,' she said firmly.

III

We had already considered, reconsidered and re-reconsidered, but we duly considered once again and came to the conclusion that the sooner we could get this done, the better our lives would be. As soon as the month was over, we were back at the ACA, registering for adoption. It was a long process and not exactly simple.

First there was the form itself – an autobiographical sketch of each parent. It asked a lot of interesting questions, neatly categorized into various sections. There was a section concerning each parent's childhood, relationship with parents, hobbies, interests, self-perception and so on. There was a separate section dealing with your married life, again asking for details like what you like in your spouse, how you make decisions with your spouse, how you express negative feelings to each other and so on. There were the more 'usual' sections dealing with income and employment, and health. There was a section on what made you consider adoption and your perception of adoption; another soliciting your views on parenting and childcare; and one enquiring about your home and neighbourhood.

It was not an easy form to fill – it required time, introspection and honesty.

In fact, you could not actually 'fill out' the form; there were no blank spaces. You had to use a separate sheet to write your answers. Laveena assured us that we could do this on the computer and email it to her, which was a relief. We both 'filled out' our forms separately, and then compared notes to see where we differed.

Next, we started to compile the documents required. Most were routine and easy to get – salary certificates, educational qualifications, date of birth and marriage certificates, proof of identity and residence and the like. There was a routine medical exam to be done by each of us, and a medical certificate to be given certifying that we were fit to adopt. In addition to all of this, we had to give letters from three people who had known us for a long time (not family members), stating that we were fit to be parents.

This was quite awkward. It wasn't that we didn't know people who would write these for us; it's just that it is quite strange to ask your friends to write a letter saying what wonderful people you are and how you'd make such fantastic parents, if only somebody would entrust you with their child.

Awkwardness notwithstanding, we got our letters. It was quite funny, really.

As soon as we heard of this requirement, and because we were now quite eager to get our documents together and get the process started, I called my dear friend Christina, and asked her if she would do this for me. Of course she would. I explained what was needed, and by the end of the week, I had a letter that was so glowing in its description of us and our potential parenting abilities that it was positively embarrassing. What was worse was that Christina had obviously thought carefully about what to say and meant every word of it. Even she was slightly embarrassed – she handed me the letter in a closed envelope and instructed me not to read it until after we had parted.

Sridhar and Sowmya were the next to give us their letter. It was just as warm and sincere. Sowmya told us that Sridhar had agonized over it for ages, framing each sentence several times over before getting it to his satisfaction.

Vyom and Vipra's letter was the best of all. Vyom declared that he had no idea how to go about it, so all four of us actually sat and drafted it together, and then, once everyone was happy with it, Vipra wrote it out neatly in her best handwriting and Vyom signed it.

Once we had all our documents neatly assembled, we went off to the ACA for the third time, to deliver the documents and set a date for the home study. The date was set for sometime in the middle of July. With this out of the way, we decided to pack our bags and head to the Himalayas for another trek. After all, with any luck, this might be our last trek before our baby came home.

IV

As soon as we got back from our trek in Ladakh, Sridhar and Sowmya invited us home for dinner. Drinks were served, but, curiously, Sowmya was not drinking any alcohol.

'Why aren't you drinking?' I asked, suspiciously.

There was an expectant pause, then Sridhar announced, 'We're expecting a baby!' So that explained the large quantities of pomegranate lying on the dining table.

For the first time in years, this announcement didn't hurt so badly. My smile was genuine, and my congratulations hearty. At last, I didn't grudge other people this happiness – we were now expecting our own baby, albeit in a rather different way.

'So your baby will come before ours,' said Amit to Sowmya, avoiding my eye. But that was okay too. It wasn't a race – any more. Ours would come when she came, now it was only a matter of time.

It was such a relief knowing that our baby would eventually come home that I had even begun to pick up the threads of friendship with those of our friends who already had babies. Vidit was just a year old, and I didn't feel I had to avoid him or his happy parents any more. I'd made my peace with Priya and met her baby too. Pregnancy in our friends' circle still caused a twinge of pain, but now it was much more manageable than it had been. Pregnancy, I told myself, wasn't everything. Mostly, it was a means to an end; and I was going to have that end by an alternative means, so that was all right. Sort of.

So while Sowmya set about enjoying her pregnancy, we looked forward to our home study. We both took the day off and drove towards the ACA together to pick up Laveena. On the drive home, conversation was neutral. I was a little nervous – it felt a bit like a test – but I felt sure it was a test that we would pass. We had everything a family could need, only the baby was missing; surely anyone could see that.

In the end, it was a fairly straightforward affair. Laveena asked us lots of questions, right from our place of birth to current income and everything in between. She wanted to know about every job either of us had ever had and everything we had ever studied. She took a good two hours over all this, and ended with a quick guided tour of the premises, which had been scrupulously tidied up in anticipation. Before she left, she asked if we had any questions, and explained a bit more about the process of adoption from here on.

'We have monthly meetings of adoptive and potential

adoptive parents,' she said. 'It would be good if you could join in one of those, so that you can talk to others who have already adopted.'

'I've already spoken to some people who have adopted,' I said.

'Other potential adoptive parents will also be there, and some of the adopted children, it will be a good experience,' she said mildly. 'But it's up to you.'

'So what happens next?' asked Amit.

'I'll write the home study report and submit it, and then you will be on the waiting list. When we have a match for you, we will call you,' she explained. 'But don't expect that we can find a baby who really looks like you or anything. We usually just match the preferences, like if you want a boy or a girl, or if you want a baby born at some particular time.'

'Oh, we're not particular about any of that,' I said quickly. 'Anything is okay, as long as the child is healthy.'

'But twins would be nice,' Amit chipped in.

When we had filled up the application form on our second visit to the ACA, we had decided to put twins as our first preference. It wasn't an impulsive action – I knew that I wanted two children, and twins held a special charm for me. Whenever I walked past a twin stroller, I always peeked in enviously and wished they could be mine. This way, we would have our whole family, and we wouldn't have to go through the whole process of adoption again. More importantly, the twins would have each other. I had read enough about how adopted children often feel a sense of isolation and a longing to search for their origins, their biological parents. Maybe with twins, some of that 'genetic' isolation would be less, maybe they would feel comforted knowing that at least they shared each other's genes.

So we'd optimistically put twins as our first preference.

Laveena looked doubtful. 'It's very rare,' she said.

'Of course, I'm sure it must be, but if you do hear of twins, keep us in mind.'

'I'll do that. Do you prefer boy–girl...'

'Any combination is fine,' I interrupted quickly. 'Boy–girl, boy–boy, girl–girl, anything is fine.'

She smiled at our eagerness. 'Any other preferences?'

'A very young baby,' I said, hesitantly. 'Three or four months old, if that's possible.' I had read that if you worked at it, it was even possible to breastfeed an adopted child. I certainly intended to try.

'The baby is going to be at least six or eight months old by the time you get her,' said Laveena. 'There are so many processes we have to complete before we give the child to the adoptive parents, so it is very difficult to have a baby younger than six months.'

I had read about the process – searching for the biological parents, giving the mother time to change her mind, all of that. All of it was to protect the interests of the child and the biological mother, there was no doubt about that. But did it have to take so long?

'Once we get a match, we will call you,' continued Laveena. 'So if you are going to be out of town or something, you should let me know beforehand. You have to say within a couple of days if you are interested, then you can see the baby.'

'And then what?' I asked eagerly.

'Generally we don't encourage parents to reject a baby unless they have a very valid reason. If parents reject a baby once or twice, it takes more time to show them another baby. Once you decide that you want the baby, then you can take her for the medical tests the same day or the next day. After you get the results, if you are satisfied, you can take the baby home.'

'Right away? What about the paperwork?' asked Amit.

'Oh, that will follow,' I answered with assurance; the other adoptive parents I had spoken to had told me this.

'The legal documents will be filed in the court after that,' Laveena added. 'It usually takes four or five months for the process to be completed. You will have to appear in court with the baby once or twice.'

That seemed too far away to be worth thinking about. Right now, all we had to do was wait.

V

Laveena also suggested that we contact adoption agencies in other states. 'Some states might have more babies and fewer parents on the waiting list, so it might work out faster,' she said.

Earlier we had been warned against registering in more than one place, so I checked again with her.

'You can't register in more than one place, whether it's with an agency or the ACA,' she explained. 'You should register only in one place and a registered social worker like me will be appointed to do the home study. Those agencies that don't have a registered social worker get the social worker from the ACA itself. The home study has to be done in the city where you are resident, so even if you register for adoption in some other state, the request will be sent by that ACA and your home study will be done by Karnataka ACA only. But once your home study is done, you can enquire in other states and other agencies. If they have a baby for you, they will contact us for the home study report and we will coordinate with them.'

It sounded complicated, but anything was worth a shot if it meant getting our baby home sooner. So the following week, I hopefully rang up agencies and ACAs in Kolkata, Chandigarh, Haryana, Punjab and Delhi. Nobody was very cooperative. Even though Haryana and Punjab were reported to have very high numbers of abandoned girl babies, they still maintained there was a long waiting list of parents. Moreover, they weren't very eager to work on an out-of-state adoption. Kolkata was equally stand-offish. 'We give preference to parents who are living in West Bengal,' I was told haughtily. Even the Missionaries of Charity in Kolkata referred me back to their Bangalore mission.

In the end, I gave up and resigned myself to a long wait.

In the meantime, for a variety of reasons, both personal and professional, I decided to quit my job. I didn't look for another one right away. I couldn't decide whether I should look for another job and try to get settled in before the baby arrived, or whether I should just wait it out and go back to work only after we had our baby. Of one thing I was quite sure: initially, for an unspecified period of time, but probably at least for a few months after the baby came home, I didn't want to work. Some companies, including my erstwhile organization, do provide maternity leave for adoption, but I didn't want that to be a criterion while searching for a job. So in the end, I decided I'd just stay home for a while. I was beginning to quite look forward to it.

Then, on my penultimate day at work, it happened. I got a call from Amit. He sounded very excited in an extremely subdued way.

'I got the call,' he whispered urgently.

'Which call?' I asked. I didn't know he had been expecting any particular call.

'*The* call,' he replied in exasperation. 'Wait, I'm searching for an empty conference room.'

In the moments it took him to find an empty conference room, the penny dropped.

'Oh, do you mean, *the* call?' I gasped.

'Yes,' he said, as I heard him close the door of what must have been an empty conference room. 'I was in the middle of an important meeting,' he went on (he was almost *always* in the middle of an important meeting in those days), 'and I got the call. I saw it was from Laveena, and I jumped up and left the room.'

'Go on. What is it?' I asked impatiently.

'They've got twins!'

'What? Twins?'

'Yes! Yes, twins! She asked me if we are interested.'

'*Of course* we are interested,' I said right away.

'That's what I told her. But she told me to think it over, talk to you and then get back to her.'

'Okay, you've talked to me, you can get back to her now,' I said, promptly.

'They're thirteen months old, both girls,' said Amit.

That made me hesitate ... for a split second. Thirteen months? Then they were past being babies. What were thirteen-month-old kids like? Would they be walking already? Talking? Would they have a personality?

'Is that okay?' asked Amit anxiously.

'Fine. Perfect. Are they healthy?'

'Yes, she said they are healthy. I'll ask her again. By the way, they're in Pondicherry,' said Amit. And with that, he rang off.

SIX

Meeting the Twins

I

The next few days passed in an agony of suspense, excitement, apprehension and fear. We were both tremendously excited at the prospect of becoming parents to twin girls, but my greatest fear was that someone, somehow, would get to them before us and take our girls away. After checking the basic facts with Laveena on the phone and reconfirming that there were, indeed, twin girls in Pondicherry up for adoption, that they were healthy and that they were almost thirteen months old, the first thing I asked her was whether we could be sure that they would not be given away to anyone else.

'No, no,' said Laveena reassuringly, 'the Tamil Nadu ACA contacted us because they have not been able to place these twins in Pondicherry or Tamil Nadu till date. As you had specifically requested for twins, we contacted you first. No other potential adoptive parents will be allowed to see the babies until you have seen them.'

'So, when can we go?' we asked.

'Let me work things out, I'll get back to you,' she said. 'Meanwhile, you can prepare yourself, if you need to make any changes or buy certain things. In case you accept the babies, you can bring them back from Pondicherry right away after the medical tests are done.'

Prepare ourselves? We didn't have a clue where to start. Most new mothers have newborn babies. Their needs are different. For food, there's breast milk. They don't move much and don't need much to play with. With thirteen-month-old babies, it's a different story. What would they eat? Drink? Wear? Play with? I called a friend, Manasi, who had a two-year-old daughter, for help.

'Twins!' she exclaimed. 'Wow! How are you going to manage?'

'I have no clue,' I answered. 'You'll have to tell me, first of all – what do I need to take just to bring them home from Pondicherry.'

'How are you going to get back?' she asked.

'Probably by taxi, I suppose. Or maybe the overnight bus. Train connections don't really work for Pondicherry,' I said. We planned on getting there by overnight bus, but that part would be easy.

'By taxi? Do you have any idea how difficult it is to manage kids in a car? Long distance? I can hardly manage one, let alone two.'

I pointed out that we didn't have too many options. Manasi actually offered to come with us to help us manage the babies, but I knew it would be difficult for her. In retrospect, I'm glad that it was just the two of us; having anyone else along, even a good friend or a family member, would have been an intrusion.

Manasi helped me draw up a list of stuff we would need:

Blankets

Towels

Night clothes – two sets each

Day clothes – two sets each (at a bare minimum, which is as far as we were going right now)

Shoes ('Though they won't really be walking yet,' said Manasi, 'but at least you can make them stand on the ground.')

Diapers, wipes and changing mats

Plastic bedsheets

Tooth brushes

Comb or brush for hair

Teethers

Toys

Bibs

Bottles (four at least), nipples and a bottle brush

'I have some of Aabha's old stuff, let me come and drop it off with you,' said Manasi. She did, and left us with a whole lot of invaluable advice as well.

The one thing she didn't tell me, and I didn't know, was that diaper sizes depend on the weight of the baby.

It was quite funny when Amit and I walked into the baby shop. We were both a little self-conscious; we didn't know anything about one-year-olds – I didn't even know, back then, what teethers were. When the shop assistant showed us clothes and shoes, we had no idea whether they would fit or be too big or too small. Everything looked tiny. The only thing we really knew for sure was that we were looking for girls' clothes.

Then we asked for diapers.

'What size,' asked the assistant.

'One-year-olds,' I said for the umpteenth time. 'Thirteen months, actually.'

'What size diapers do you need? Medium or large? What is the baby's weight?' asked the sales assistant.

Amit and I looked at each other blankly. Weight? We didn't know their weight. Laveena had read out some numbers to us indicating their height and weight at their last check-up a few months ago. The numbers hadn't even registered.

'Let's skip the diapers,' said Amit. 'We can buy them in Pondicherry. We might not even need them, after all.'

Yes, that was the difficult bit. Much as we were thrilled

to bits at the prospect of twins, we had to keep reminding ourselves that this might not actually work out after all. I still had this horrible suspicion that we might find, when we reached, that some other couple, perhaps with the right connections, had beaten us to it. Amit, more practically, pointed out that the medical tests could reveal something that might force us to reconsider. Secretly, I felt that only a very serious medical condition would hold me back. I was quite determined to make these twins mine – if only they would wait till we got to them.

II

We first heard of the twins on 13 September 2007. In just a week, everything was fixed up for us to actually go to Pondicherry, and we reached on the morning of 22 September. We had bought and carried along almost everything that Manasi had suggested, apart from the diapers. We even had a couple of bulky toys that she had passed on to us. Back at home, I'd been on a tidying-up spree, removing all the breakables from the lower shelves of the kitchen cabinets and rearranging some of the bedroom cupboards. I put away glass tumblers and took out steel ones. China plates were packed up and replaced with melamine. Breakable and treasured knick-knacks were hidden away. The cupboard in the guest bedroom was ruthlessly emptied of all the junk that it had accumulated over the years. It was a lot of work, and I did it only because I felt that, *if* we brought the twins home with us, I wouldn't have the time and energy to do any of this then.

But I didn't make too many changes, and we didn't buy anything much ... just in case...

We had been to Pondicherry once before, with a large group of friends. We'd stayed in Auroville then, done all the touristy things, had a lot of fun. We hadn't spent much time in Pondicherry itself, apart from a brief visit to the Promenade. It had been a short, busy weekend trip. We'd never dreamt that we'd be coming back here on such a different mission.

I love to travel, to get to know new places, to ferret out their secrets and to experience their individuality. But this time I paid no attention whatsoever to this new place that I found myself in. I saw the street signs – there's JIPMER (the Jawaharlal Institute of Postgraduate Medical Education and Research), where the twins were born; there's the ubiquitous MG Road; this one is Anna Salai, and so on – and I tried to get my bearings with regard to the road going to the agency and the road going to the bus stand. But I didn't get, or even try to get, any sense of the place. Pondicherry was no longer just a tourist destination for me. It became, instead, the place where my kids were born and a place I visited later on too many times, for the paperwork and legalities surrounding the adoption.

Earlier, when we had briefly considered adopting from Kolkata, we were told by someone that the adopted baby couldn't leave the state for six months. We had considered how feasible it would be for me to stay with the baby in Kolkata, while Amit returned to Bangalore to work. When it turned out that we'd be adopting from Pondicherry, we were less concerned. Surely they'd allow the babies to go as far as Tamil Nadu, and Tamil Nadu was hardly an hour's drive from Bangalore. Perhaps I could rent a small place in Hosur or somewhere nearby, and Amit could come to visit every weekend.

'But just think,' said Christina, when I discussed it with her, 'you could actually spend six months in Pondicherry. That would be so nice.'

It would have been, perhaps, in a way. But I knew that, more than staying in a peaceful, pleasant place, I'd value having friends, family and a familiar environment around me. Luckily, though, it turned out that the six-month rule did not apply in our case.

As soon as we got off at the Pondicherry bus stand, we took an auto to the agency. It was a little outside town. We rattled along a minor highway, then we turned off it and got lost in a maze of narrow streets. Amit called the agency and the Sister there spoke to the auto driver on the phone and gave him directions. We went down a long, winding road, with intermittent poor-looking houses on one side. There was a signboard at the corner of an impossibly narrow turn, which looked more like a driveway than a road. The auto turned into it, and just a little ahead was our agency, sweetly called Joy Home.

On the left of the road was a small house with a tiny, paved yard in front. There were a few chairs, a few kids and a few dogs about. On the right was a larger building, with a front porch and a comfortable hallway visible through the open doors. We went in and were shown to Sister Rosemary's office. Greetings and comments of an introductory nature were exchanged, and tea was served.

Very soon, the twins were brought in by two caregivers, and handed to each of us.

III

There may be people who hold their adopted babies for the very first time and know right away that this is their baby. I am not one of them. I looked at the twins and I *knew* that they were somebody else's babies.

I used to think that the very first time I held my adopted daughter – I didn't know then that we'd have twins – there would be some magic. I expected to feel something soft … something tender, maternal, loving. I felt sure that it wouldn't matter that it was someone else's child I was holding, that the child would straightaway feel like mine, ours. I thought I'd feel happy, ecstatic even, and most of all, I thought I'd feel sure. Confident. I was confident that I'd be confident ... when the time came.

But I was nothing of the sort. What I was, was determined. I was determined to be a mother to these two children. But right then, there wasn't much motherly feeling in me. I felt two steps removed from the scene – like watching someone else clumsily taking hold of someone else's baby.

My first impression was that the twins were *dark*. Laveena had told us they were medium-complexioned, not fair, but not too dark. To me, they looked dark, quite dark. But I had already made up my mind on this. I was *not* – regardless of any rooted preference or suppressed bias, regardless of the bias pervasive in our society and regardless of how our own biological child *might* have been, if it had ever been – I was absolutely *not* going to hold the colour of its skin against any baby.

They both had snub, upturned noses, long eyelashes and full, heavy upper lips that almost entirely engulfed their lower lips. Their hair, which was silky and dark but not jet black, was in a pretty dreadful condition. It looked as if it had been butchered, instead of barbered. (Later I saw that apparently all the kids in the agency had been subjected to the ministrations of the same butcher, I mean, barber.) They had the thickly flowing, snotty noses that

I had, with a mixture of disgust and resignation, already subconsciously come to associate with very small kids. They had on nondescript frocks that looked a bit ragged, with a hankie pinned to the front, and they were barefoot.

At that first meeting, I could not really read their expressions. They were still, after all, somebody else's babies that I was studying, and I was certainly no expert on babies and their various moods and expressions. Looking back at photographs of that first day, the first few moments, I feel now that they wore expressions of fear combined with unhappiness – or at least, if not actual unhappiness, an absence of happiness. At that time, I would probably have described their expressions as wary – but then, this was only to be expected when two small children are suddenly entrusted to two complete strangers who are themselves not entirely confident about handling those children.

Those expressions of fear and lack of happiness took a long time to fade completely from their faces. They remained cautious and slightly clingy and scared-looking creatures outside our home for many months after coming to us. So it was with great joy and (unjustified) pride that we watched them bloom, gradually, and without conscious effort on our part, into two confident, outgoing, cheerful little girls. This transition might have been less apparent to others – it might even have been a natural and inevitable phase of their babyhood – but to us it was an achievement, even a victory of sorts.

A friend told me once that I was reading too much into this change. 'All babies are quiet and shy at that age,' he said. 'Why, our own daughter was so quiet at that age, everyone commented on it. But look at her now.'

I didn't think that all children had the same extent and the same expression of quietness, insecurity and placidity that our kids had had. But I wouldn't know. Part of being an adoptive parent is not knowing what your child would have been like if she had not been adopted; if you had been the one to carry her and give birth to her; if you had been there with her and held her and cared for her in that first hour, first day, first week, first whole year of her life. Perhaps she would have been no different. Or perhaps she would have been quite different. You will never know.

I spoke to my mother on the phone, telling her about the kids. There was so little to say.

'They look okay. They have long eyelashes. They are quite dark,' I said.

'No, it doesn't bother me,' I replied with determination.

'I guess they are healthy – at least ... well, they have colds, and one of them has these scars, but apart from that...' Apart from that, I wouldn't know until we got the all-clear from the medical tests.

I hung up and looked at the babies again. They were rather smaller than I had expected. Not having had much experience with kids at all, the mental image I'd had would probably have corresponded more with a three- or four-year-old than with a one-year-old. But then again, maybe they were just rather small for their age.

I'm not a person who's excessively fond of babies. I never have been, not even when I made up my mind that I wanted babies of my own. Even then, I didn't really coo over other people's babies or think them cute. So I didn't think these babies were cute either. Really, they weren't. Apart from the terribly snotty noses, there were the sores and scabs on one girl's arms and legs, and the scars on her face; there were the disastrous haircuts; and the dull, lacklustre, wary eyes. No, there was no escaping it – they weren't beautiful.

But that didn't matter. What mattered was: would they be mine? *Could* they be mine?

As Amit and I held them, and they wailed, wanting to go back to their familiar caregivers, I began to feel cautiously optimistic. They were real. Nobody else had snatched them away from us so far. Now that I could hold them, I wouldn't *let* anyone snatch them away. Yes, they would be mine – if only the medical tests gave us the all-clear.

At that point, we found it difficult to differentiate between the twins. Helpfully, the staff pointed out one or two very minor differentiating features. Even so, I continued to get confused between which one was which for the first few days. By the time we had them in the car on the road back to Bangalore, I had got it straight and was determinedly memorizing it. *This* was Mrinalinee, Inmathy.

That was Nayantara, Illavarasi. Amit and I checked and rechecked with each other, till we had both finally got it.

We had, of course, come prepared with names of our own. Someone, at some point, had mentioned that we'd need to fill it in some form right away. But we didn't want to abandon their old names and start using the new names immediately. They needed, I felt, in the middle of this huge change in their lives, at least the familiarity of the names they were used to.

IV

It was Saturday afternoon already, so we had to rush to get their medical tests done, so that we could get the results on Sunday morning. We had lunch at Joy Home, in the house across the street. The room was small and dark, but it was clean and the food was simple and tasty. The person from the Tamil Nadu ACA ate with us, then he left. The twins had been whisked away for lunch as well. Casual enquiries revealed that they were used to 'normal' food – rice, idli, sambar, fish, egg, curd. That at least was a relief, I thought.

The agency arranged a car for us, and two attendants came along with the twins. One of them spoke English; we didn't know a word of Tamil between the two of us, so we did need an interpreter.

The entire time that we spent taking the twins to the hospital, getting various tests done in various departments and taking them back again early in the evening, Amit and I made it a point to hold them and carry them around as much as possible, swapping babies every so often. We were keen to get both of them accustomed to us while they still had familiar faces around to comfort them. Soon, they would be torn away from everything that was known and comforting. They didn't know what was in store and so, perhaps, couldn't fear it, but we knew and I was apprehensive on their behalf.

They didn't seem to mind being carried by us as long as they could see their caregivers around. They made no overtures towards us, though – there was no eye contact, no real holding on to us. For my part, I still felt as though I was carrying somebody else's children. In my mind I knew that these children might become ours, but just then, physically, each one was an unfamiliar object. I arranged them this way and that, trying to get used to them. Maybe it was as much a matter of getting used to the thought of holding them, as it was about the physical effort of holding them.

The hospital that the agency habitually used was PIMS (the Pondicherry Institute of Medical Sciences), and the twins already had immunization cards in their name there, so it was there that we took them for their medical tests. The first thing that happened was that their weight and height was measured, and then we were in queue to meet a paediatrician. After a long, tedious wait, our turn came, and we went in and sat down. Amit held one girl, I had the other, and I presented each to the doctor in turn.

The first thing we told the doctor was that we were adopting the twins, and she apparently knew what to do.

'They are generally okay,' she told us, as she examined them in turn. 'But they are quite small for their age.' Their birthweight, she noted, was about 2.75 kg. 'Most babies triple their birthweight in the first year,' she explained. I did the math quickly and thought they should be about 8.5 kg. Or, that's what they should have been a month ago. Tara was 7.25 kg, and Mrini was a little better at 7.75 kg. So they were only about a kilo or so off. Was that so bad?

'They are now in the bottom fifth percentile,' the doctor added.

That sounded worrying.

'It's nothing to worry about,' she said almost at once. 'At the agency, they do the best they can, but it is a difficult job. Once they come into a stable family environment, they'll improve.'

The word 'malnutrition' floated into my mind.

'It's not only about the kind of nourishment they get, it's also to do with the family aspects, love, attention and so on,' said the doctor. It was almost as if she was reading my mind. Perhaps she'd done this many times before.

She went on to prescribe a host of medicines: something for their cold, which was very apparent and quite bad, some vitamins, an iron supplement and a calcium supplement. Their immunizations, she said, were up to date and could be continued at a hospital in Bangalore.

With very young babies, tests can be done for sight and hearing, but in our case, as the girls were over a year old, it was quite clear that they could see and hear and respond to their names and make eye contact. So the main tests that we needed would be a set of blood tests. The only thing we were really concerned about was HIV. Neither of us wanted to take on the stress and heartache of coping with an HIV-positive child. Amit was also worried about thalassemia and other nameless congenital conditions, but I was prepared to cope with ailments that were not seriously disabling. We had had, in fact, a fairly serious debate on the matter before we left Bangalore, eventually agreeing that we would cross that bridge when, and if, we came to it.

Getting the blood for the blood test was a nightmarish experience. For some reason, the doctors insisted that I – not one of the accompanying caregivers, who might have been more experienced at this – should be the one to hold the babies down as they tried to get the blood out of their veins. I am not normally squeamish at such things, but holding a hollering baby down was something I'd never done before. And getting blood out of the veins is not a simple job. Mrini started screaming blue murder long before the needle came anywhere near her skin. She could be heard all along the corridor. She was so hysterical that, in the end, I took her out and deposited her with the attendants, who gave her a bottle of warm milk, while I took Tara in.

Tara also howled, but nothing like Mrini. When I took her out after it was done, she soon settled down, but when I took Mrini back, it was just as bad as it had been before. With me and a nurse holding her down with all our might, another nurse finally managed to stick the needle in, but she continued to howl and scream long after it was all done.

Bad as it was being in on this experience, it must have been even worse for Amit, who was sitting outside and having visions of death and disaster being inflicted on the tiny creature.

The only other department we had to go to was paediatric dermatology. It was, at that point, news to me that dermatology came in a paediatric flavour. I left Tara with Amit, who had the onerous task of delivering the blood samples to the HIV lab, while I took Mrini up to paediatric dermatology. There, I showed Mrini's arms and legs, which were liberally covered in some kind of insect bite or rash, to a young junior doctor. She gave me a bit of a scare, because, after being told of the context, her initial comment was that it could be syphilis.

Syphilis!

All I knew about syphilis was that it was a sexually transmitted disease. That it could also be passed on to babies at birth was not surprising. But syphilis in babies, said my mother when I told her of it, could be serious. Very serious, in fact, especially if it had been left untreated for over a year.

A senior doctor was called in, and he decided that it certainly wasn't syphilis. 'Do you know what scabies is?' he asked me.

'Isn't it what happens to dogs?'

Apparently it was not quite the same thing. 'It's a kind of mite,' he said. 'It's nothing to worry about.'

That was a relief.

He gave us a prescription for a cream. 'You have to apply this all over the body, for her and for all the people in the family. Use the full tube for each person. Leave it on overnight. The next morning, you have to wash all her clothes and bedclothes. Repeat the treatment after a week.'

That didn't sound too bad. I did it a few days after we got home and realized that it was, in fact, very tedious and very tiring. There was so much to be washed, and in the perpetually overcast and rainy weather that we were having (the tail end of the monsoon), everything took forever to dry. I actually did the treatment thrice, not twice, because the rash seemed to come back some days after the second treatment. But eventually it did go away and Mrini's skin started to improve.

It was late afternoon when we got into the hired car and headed back to the agency that Saturday. It must have been one of the few occasions on which the twins had travelled by car, and considering that they'd just had a bottle full of warm milk, it shouldn't have surprised us that at least one of them should puke all over us. Disgusting as it was to be covered in semi-curdled-milk puke, I told myself that it was only to be expected and I held her close and comforted her. It was the start of a lasting bond.

V

The agency had booked us into a fairly decent hotel in Pondicherry. Once we had returned the babies to the agency, we went to the hotel without wasting any time. They must have been disgusted by us when we checked in – I still had vomit on my clothes.

We were exhausted! Sister Rosemary had in fact urged us to take the twins to the hotel with us and keep them overnight. We both were a little surprised by her eagerness on this count, but we were not emotionally, mentally, or physically prepared to manage the babies that night. Besides, we still didn't want to get too close to these girls, until we had the all-clear from the medical tests, so we quickly declined.

It was a strange evening and night. Exhausted as we were, there were phone calls to make, friends and family to inform and consult. I don't think I had any time to get my own jumbled thoughts and emotions straightened out. I was no longer happy or excited – those seemed like trivial emotions now. I was anxious that the medical reports should be clear; apprehensive about the logistics of getting the babies home; and nervous, or perhaps just plain terrified, at the enormity of what we were about to take on. Could I really manage these two unknown babies? I didn't know anything about babies. What was I getting in to? Right now, we could still turn around and catch the next bus home. But if we took these babies home with us tomorrow, there would be no going back. Were we doing the right thing?

At that time I think I didn't even want to admit it to myself, but deep down, I was scared.

For the longest time, we had thought that when we got our baby, we'd celebrate. We'd have a grand meal out, a five-course dinner with drinks and dessert – just the two of us. We didn't realize it, but if we had really wanted to celebrate with a grand meal, we should have done it then, on that Saturday night. The next day onwards, we had absolutely no scope for celebration – for a long, long, long time to come.

As it was, we were so tired, we just ate something in our room and fell into bed.

The next morning, we were back at the agency at 9 a.m. A urine and stool test had been recommended, but we were too late. The urine had been passed without being collected, the stool had been collected from one girl but not the other. 'She hasn't given a sample,' was the explanation we were given. The samples should have reached the lab within half an hour of being collected, so the one sample that they had managed to collect was already stale.

'We'll just have to do it in Bangalore,' Amit said. I nodded – how bad could a routine stool and urine test result be, anyway?

We picked up the girls and their attendants and drove all the way back to PIMS to collect the medical reports. Thankfully they were all clear. The blood test indicated anaemia, but the doctor's opinion was that a balanced diet and some iron supplement would soon fix that. HIV, our biggest concern, was thankfully negative. In fact, Laveena had told us that the twins had already been tested for HIV and were negative, but it was the one test that we were most determined to have done again. Now that that was confirmed negative, there were no obstacles to the adoption.

Even now, there was no euphoria in me – only a grateful, half-scared realization that now we could take our babies, go home and start, at last, on our own journey of parenting.

We started on the long drive back to the agency, when I noticed that the girls weren't wearing 'anything'. That is, they were fully clothed, of course, but they didn't have any diaper or nappy-type thing on underneath. They were sitting on our laps – Amit's and mine. I'd had one round of puke on me already the previous day and had no desire to risk anything else. We asked the driver to stop at a suitable shop as soon as possible and Amit rushed off to buy diapers. In the moving car, with the attendants looking on approvingly, we managed for the first time (the first of about a million times) to put a diaper each on our babies.

'Okay, that wasn't so bad, we can do this,' we said to each other once both the babies had been diapered up. Of course, we hadn't had to handle a dirty diaper yet, but we had plenty of opportunity to do that too, soon enough. We also didn't know that we had managed to put the diaper on backwards, with the sticky tabs at the back – we only realized that a few days later when I actually read the instructions on the diaper packet. But the diaper did its job well enough anyway, which was the important thing.

Back at the agency again, I tried to find out what kind of schedule the twins were used to. When did they eat, sleep, play? What did they eat? Drink? The staff were strangely reluctant to give us detailed information. Perhaps they simply didn't think it important. 'They eat everything,' was the general, cheerful response.

We discussed paperwork. We had seen the agency's file on the twins, but we hadn't got copies of the releavant documents. 'We'll send you everything by post,' Sister Rosemary assured us.

They also needed further documents from us. The process seemed to differ slightly in Pondicherry compared to what we had been told for Karnataka, so we would have to supply some additional documents, including an undertaking from a family member that they would look after our adopted children in case of any eventuality. 'You can send everything by post after you get back to Bangalore,' Sister Rosemary assured us.

There was a brief 'ceremony' – for want of a better word – of handing the babies to us. We were told to put fresh clothes on them. The agency kept whatever the twins had been wearing so far. They had on two cheap plastic bangles on each hand, and these were left on. (Months later, I took these off and kept them away safely as the only mementos of the whole first year of their lives.) I had neglected to carry hankies (which speaks volumes for how ill-prepared we were), so we were given a hankie apiece, but that was all. Then we all went into the front hall, where there was a brief prayer. Then the twins were ceremoniously handed over to us, and various members of the staff came to wish them goodbye.

Next, we needed a foster-care agreement to be drawn up, that would allow us to take the twins away with us. The agency facilitated the process, getting it typed on stamp paper and attested by a notary public the same afternoon. They also helped us to book a taxi for our return to Bangalore the next morning.

By early evening, we were back in our hotel room – with our two little girls this time. What the hotel staff thought of us – one day adorned in vomit, the next day walking in with two babies who obviously didn't belong to us – I'd rather not know. No eyebrows were raised, at least not overtly; perhaps they'd hosted adoptive parents before us.

Amit was on the phone almost the entire evening, informing people, receiving congratulations. He passed the phone to me every so often, and I took it, hardly registering whom I was talking to, hardly hearing what they asked, hardly knowing what to say. I was tired and completely preoccupied with our babies. What would I need next? Food? Milk? Water? Diapers? Medicines? I watched them sleep and wondered how I would manage when they woke up. Then I remembered all those trips to maternity wards to visit friends who'd just delivered; I remembered watching their exhausted, but blissful, expressions with envy. Now, at last, I was there. I might never have been pregnant, I might never have been in labour, I might be in a hotel room instead of a maternity ward, and I might have got thirteen-month-olds, instead of a newborn ... but at last, I had delivered.

SEVEN

The Homecoming

I

That evening was an unmitigated disaster, and it was followed by a terrible night.

At about the time we thought the girls might want their dinner, we asked room service for hot milk. When they brought it, it was scalding hot. By the time it had cooled sufficiently, the twins were seriously hungry, howling for food. We held them in our laps and they sucked the milk out of the bottles greedily.

Then we tried some food on them. We didn't know how much they would eat and of what, but we tried idli and curd rice. I remember holding one of the girls in in my lap and Amit and I both feeding her when, at one point, she turned right around and looked straight into my eyes. It was the first time she (or either of them) had ever done that. In that moment, she seemed to accept me. She seemed, or so I fancied, to say, 'Okay, if you're going to feed me, you can't be all bad; I suppose I can live with this.'

Neither Amit nor I slept much that night. We weren't used to having babies in our bed, and were both scared of rolling over on top of them or smothering them. We weren't prepared for how restless babies are at night – the girls turned all the way around in bed, and even, at one point tried to roll off the foot of the bed.

And they dirtied the bed. How they dirtied the bed! One or both of them had diarrhoea and the diapers had not been proof against it. The next morning, as I tried to clean and change one girl, the other continued to mess. In addition to the diarrhoea, there were small instalments of vomit coming out as well. Perhaps the food had not suited them, or perhaps it was the milk. Or perhaps it was the stress, not evident in any other way. All I remember is trying to clean up faster than they dirtied – and it was a losing battle.

Our car reported punctually at 6 a.m. In anticipation of an early departure, we had been up since five. But with things going wrong at an alarming pace, it was well after 7 a.m. before we managed to get all our bits and pieces together (we had not had time to pack, really) and leave the room.

It takes about six hours to get from Pondicherry to Bangalore by road. We stopped for breakfast at some point, and got home around lunch time. The journey was much less traumatic than I thought it would be. In fact, the twins had been very, very quiet. I thought they might be visibly upset at waking up in a strange place with new faces around them and everything new and unfamiliar, but they made no mention of it. They did not know what to make of the toys we'd brought, but they sat quietly in our laps, or slept on the seat between us without fussing.

The breakfast halt was quite interesting. I felt very self-conscious, walking into a public place with two babies who looked like they did not belong to us. But there was a waiter there who immediately took to the twins and played with them and talked to them; he didn't seem to notice that they could not possibly be ours. The girls ate an idli or two each, which was encouraging, and were generally well behaved. I was terrified of two possibilities: that they would start bawling for some reason and that we would be unable to comfort them, or that somebody would call the cops saying that these could not be our babies and we'd have to defend ourselves. In the latter case, all we had to prove that we were legally sanctioned to take care of the twins was the foster-care agreement – and a very frail and flimsy document it appeared to me.

But none of this happened. Instead, something else happened. I was feeding the girls idli-sambar, and then I started to take a bite for myself. Automatically, I took a fresh spoon.

In many families, it might be normal for each person to use a separate spoon. In our family – both with my parents, as well as with Amit – we didn't bother. We used whatever plate, mug, bowl, glass, or spoon was handy (unless somebody was seriously sick – then we would try to be a little more hygienic). Using a fresh spoon was something I'd automatically do with an *outsider*. I looked at both the girls. They still looked like someone else's children. They still *felt* like someone else's children. Deliberately, I put down the fresh spoon and picked up the spoon I was using to feed her, and ate some idli with it. I had to break through these mental barriers some day, and now was a pretty good time to start.

After that, it never bothered me again.

Around the time we reached the outskirts of Bangalore, the twins became terribly hungry and demanded their bottles. We were not carrying milk, and – given the delicate condition of their stomachs that morning – we didn't want to stop at some roadside restaurant. So we committed the criminal act of filling their bottles with water. This pacified them for a few minutes, but they were hungry again soon, and I felt miserably guilty as they wailed unstoppably and as loudly as they could. But finally we made it home. They both stopped crying as the car drew up and stopped outside our building. Amit paid off the taxi, while I collected some of our scattered belongings and scooped up one of the kids in my arms.

He picked up the other girl and we headed up the steps to our apartment.

At last, our daughters had come home.

II

Being quite a private and a rather self-conscious person, the first and most immediate difficulty for me was getting past all the people who habitually hang around outside a multi-storey apartment complex – the security guards, the drivers, the corner-shop shopkeepers, the flower sellers, the car washers, the street sweepers and garbage collectors, the dhobis and all the other sundry hangers-on. They are people you walk by and – usually – nod at every day, and yet they are not friends. They need to be told that we have two new additions to our family, yet you can't call them on the phone to tell them, you don't want to discuss the details of the adoption with them, and you can't throw a big party for them. You just let them see you with the kids and draw their own conclusions.

Of course, some of them will come right out with it and ask you about the kids. In many ways, that makes it easier. In our case, it was our building manager who cornered me a day or two after we brought the girls home.

'Are these your children?' he asked.

'Yes, they are.' I didn't need to explain further – they obviously looked nothing like Amit and me, and these folks had seen me often enough for months on end to know that I had not been pregnant, and certainly not with one-year-old twins.

'I saw you carrying one child and going up, I thought you must have some guests. Then I saw your husband taking another child up, she looked just like the one you carried,' he said. 'Are they twins?'

'Yes, they are.'

'Yes, they look just identical.'

I smiled politely and waited for the next question, which was clearly on the way.

'Where did you get them?'

'From Pondicherry. We adopted them.'

'Okay.' Pause. 'How much did you pay?'

After that, word got around and these conversations became fewer and fewer as people got accustomed to seeing us together with our babies.

As soon as we got home, we gave the girls their milk and put them down on the mattress in their room. Tara fell asleep right away, but Mrini decided she wasn't sleepy after all. She got up, crawled to the open door, smiled, and set about exploring her new home with curiosity and apparent delight. It was amazing and very touching to see how quickly she started to find her feet. The kitchen and dining room were soon part of their extended territory, and the other bedroom and living room were added to the map in a couple of days.

I got busy cooking dinner for the girls and trying to organize our home for them. They were not yet tall enough to reach things kept on the dining table or kitchen counter, but there were several plug points that were conveniently within their reach, and many doors that they could pinch their fingers in. There were some glass-fronted bookshelves that were clearly dangerous, and a rocking chair that was simply asking for trouble. We moved stuff around so that most of the dangerous items were closed off in the study, which now began to look like a junk yard. We added an extra mattress in our bedroom and tried to tell ourselves that it was spacious enough for all of us. It wasn't.

We hadn't, of course, bought them a crib or a cot or a play pen or anything fancy like that. That was due to the endless uncertainty of the adoption process – you don't know how old your baby is going to be, when she is going to come home, and you just never know, right up until it has happened, whether it is going to work out or not.

With pregnancy, it's not as if there are no risks, but the timeline is somewhat clearer and, depending on the mother's age, health, and medical situation, you might have good reason to be optimistic. Plus, you know that when your baby comes, it will be a newborn baby, with all that goes along with that. With adoption, you just can't know. You might know what sex your baby will be (usually a girl, unless otherwise specified), but you don't know what age your baby will be, so you can't buy age-appropriate clothes, toys, bedding, or feeding, carrying and bathing equipment. When Sridhar and Sowmya had their baby six months later, Sridhar had his own old carved wooden cot, carefully repaired and polished, placed next to their bed. Sowmya managed to get hold of a beautiful old wickerwork bassinet with brand new pretty frilly cloth covers tailor-made in both pink and blue, so that the gender-appropriate colour could be slipped on without delay. All we had in the early days was the few essentials we'd bought before we left for Pondicherry, a cluttered spare bedroom, the same old mattress on the floor that we'd always had, insufficient cupboard space and a house that was woefully lacking in child-proofing for two one-year-olds who were already crawling with gusto and would soon learn to walk. Even our tiny old fridge was no longer good enough for a family of four with two starkly different sets of food and drink requirements. All of these deficiencies would have to be tackled soon, with varying degrees of urgency.

Meanwhile, I tried to work out what they would eat, and when, and how. I didn't yet have any parenting books, so I just took Manasi's advice – thin dal, overcooked rice, boiled potatoes, bananas. They didn't eat much, and what they did came out fluidly from both ends. The second day, Monday, I tried milk followed by boiled egg and rice kheer on them at dinner time. They ate with gusto and vomited it all out a few minutes later, when I was holding one of them in my lap. Immediately, the doorbell rang. Great: there was vomit all over the floor, all over me, and all over the kids… and we had guests.

At this stage, we had not yet got our domestic help organized. We had a cook who came in the evening, and her sister who came once a week, usually on Saturday morning, to clean the house. I had not said anything to either of them about the adoption, 'just in case'. So on Monday evening, when our cook, NJ, came to work, she was amazed to see the twins. I explained to her about the adoption and asked if she could help me manage them.

'My other employer has gone out of town this week, so this week I can come in the morning. Say, from nine till about twelve. But next week I have to go back to the other place,' she said. 'You could ask my sister, she's not working anywhere else.'

I asked her to come for the one week that she was available – at that point, I couldn't think beyond a week anyway. I didn't know how to bathe the kids, I didn't know how to oil them or wash their hair. I didn't know how to brush their teeth or gums, or even whether I should be brushing them. I didn't know how to put them to bed. I didn't really even know how to feed them or burp them. I didn't know anything. One week was an eternity; I didn't even know how to get through each day right then.

I was reasonably certain even then that I didn't want to

have full-time help hanging around the house in the long run. I wanted to be the primary caregiver myself. I wanted to be the one bathing, feeding, comforting and playing with the kids. How else would I really get to know them? How else would I ever form a real bond with these two children, or they with me?

What I wasn't at all certain about was whether I *could* manage it all on my own. Was one week time enough to find out?

III

Given that I wanted to manage the twins on my own, there was never any question about whether I should establish a schedule for feeding the kids and putting them to bed, or let them take each day as it comes. There *had* to be a schedule, for my own sanity. And that schedule had to be a common one; I couldn't possibly manage two kids eating, sleeping, bathing and playing at different times. When would I ever get any housework done, to say nothing of bathing, using the toilet, or getting some rest? So for the first few days, I let the twins pick their own times for eating and napping, and after that I worked on merging their schedules. It wasn't difficult: they seemed to have a similar sort of timetable anyway and seemed to prefer to fall asleep at generally the same time each day. In a week or so, I had a rhythm going. They woke around 7 a.m. They napped at eleven in the morning, and after lunch, around three in the afternoon. They slept around 9.30 at night. They got four meals a day: breakfast, lunch, tea and dinner. They got no feed at night. Apart from general restlessness on their part, and general anxiety on our part, all four of us slept right through each night.

Luckily for me, I soon had them taking just one nap a day and retiring for the night by 8.30 p.m. What relief I felt at the end of each long day, when I closed the door behind them and collapsed with a sigh in a heap on the sofa! At least I had a couple of hours to myself now, before falling asleep and waking up, still tired, to start the whole crazy circus once again.

On Tuesday morning, with their noses still snotty and their digestion still highly volatile, we took the twins to the hospital. I wondered whether we'd have any trouble getting hospital cards made for them. We had no document certifying their birth, their link with us, or their names, other than the foster-care agreement, and I wasn't sure how much weight that would carry. But nobody asked and, in a few minutes, we had the first documentary evidence that this here was Miss Mrinalinee Mukherjee and this Miss Nayantara Mukherjee.

The paediatrician checked their immunization cards and told us which shots were pending and when we should go for them. She examined Mrini's scars and concurred that the current rash looked like scabies. An earlier rash, of which there was evidence in the form of scars, she said might have been chickenpox. Or it might not. Here was another frustration of not knowing every tiny detail of the first year of their lives: that rash could have been any kind of skin condition. Months later, when we finally got around to shaving their heads, we found that Mrini had a number of strange scars on her scalp. What could have caused those? The doctor said it might be fungal and gave us some creams and a shampoo to use, which helped to reduce it a bit. Eventually her hair covered it up, but it never went away.

The doctor prescribed a fresh set of tonics, vitamins and supplements, and recommended another couple of blood tests, along with the pending stool and urine tests. At this point, we weren't testing for any medical condition that might force us to change our minds regarding the adoption; we were past that stage. All we wanted was to ensure that our girls were in good health, and to identify and treat any conditions that could be detected.

Reluctantly, we subjected them to another blood test. It was almost as bad as the first time, but this time at least we knew what we were in for. Perhaps the doctors here were more practised too, and they got it over and done with quickly. It helped that the girls were asleep in our arms almost up until the moment when I placed them on the bed for the blood test.

Thankfully, when we got the test results a few days later, they showed that everything was okay.

The same day, with the hospital trip behind us, the blood test just a memory, and both girls rested, fed and happy, we decided to extend the outing by taking them out shopping. As soon as we'd brought the girls home, Amit had gone out and bought a few essentials, but we still needed a lot of things, big things, like a twin stroller, more clothes, shoes, toys, floor potties and – most essential – high chairs. Amit and I had been feeding them – with NJ's help at times – on our laps, but if I wanted to manage them on my own once Amit went back to office next week, I had to have high chairs to put them in. So we took them on their first shopping expedition.

In some ways, it was a difficult trip to the baby shop. For the first time, I came face-to-face with a lot of lovely baby stuff that I'd never had the opportunity to shop for. I eyed the beautiful wooden cribs and cots longingly, but our girls would soon be past that age and a mattress on the floor was safer. One thing I did buy though – I bought a baby bag: one of those multipurpose bags that you carry diapers, wipes, change of clothing, baby bottle and other baby stuff in when you want to go out. I probably didn't need it, it wasn't very practical and our girls soon outgrew it, but I bought it anyway, because I really wanted it. I had my babies at last, and I wasn't going to be denied this one potent (for me) symbol of motherhood, the baby bag. I had two girls, but they didn't have it in pink, so I bought the blue one – I wasn't going to take a chance on coming back for it later. When I finally gave it away, reluctantly, many months later, I almost cried: I hadn't ever had that time with my babies, that first year; I hadn't ever really needed that bag at all.

The twin stroller, on the other hand, was everything I had ever dreamed of. It was my answer to all the countless times I had peeped in to other people's strollers to catch a glimpse of their bubbly babies. It was, especially, my answer to all the times I had peeped into other people's twin strollers and thought, longingly, how nice it would be to have twins of my own. At last, I was the one pushing the stroller; *I* was the cynosure of all eyes! Strangers looked into *my* stroller and smiled at me, and I smiled back and felt like a million dollars. Yes, this stroller and the two lovely little girls in it were mine. They were mine!

Thinking back, I can't say when it changed. At first, they felt like not mine, and not really lovely. At some point, just a few days later, they were lovely and they were mine. I knew it, I felt it, but I have no idea how it came to be. Perhaps it was just by being with them all the time, holding them, bathing them, feeding them, playing with them. Is that what bonding is all about? All I know is that my feelings about them changed and it happened quite soon and it was effortless and completely unnoticeable.

On Monday evening, we hadn't had the energy to take

the girls out anywhere, but on Tuesday, after our successful excursion to the doctor and the baby shop in the morning, we decided to take the girls out to the park in their brand new stroller. I probably would not have had the courage to attempt such a feat alone, but Amit had none of the fears and anxieties that I was always burdened with and so we all went out together. It was a landmark occasion, not only because we continued to take the kids to the park regularly for years after that, but also because it was my first step towards overcoming the self-consciousness I felt about being seen outside with our two kids who looked so distinctly unlike us. I found out that people *would* talk to you about it, ask you about it, and that was okay. I discovered that I really didn't mind talking about it at all.

With NJ and Amit and the twin stroller and the high chairs and the park outings and the assorted doses of medicines, one week somehow went by. It was strange how at times it seemed to fly past, and at other times it just didn't seem to move at all, but ultimately it did pass. At the end of day one, I was just relieved to have got through it. At the end of the second day, I was tired. At the end of the third day, I was tired past exhaustion. We were experimenting with cloth nappies. I'd just placed each of the girls on the potty and then put them in fresh nappies for the night. (This was just three days into parenting. I still hadn't got hold of any of the fantastic parenting books on exactly when and how to potty-train your child, much less had the time to read anything on the Net on the subject. And I hadn't yet learnt from experience that cloth nappies just *don't work* unless *somebody else* is washing them.) They'd managed to mess the bedding. I changed it. They messed it again. I changed it again. At last they fell asleep. It was 10 p.m. I was faced with a mountain of stinking laundry of the kind that can't go into the washing machine. The idea of leaving it for the next morning was unthinkable. There was nothing else to do but cry.

After that, we switched to disposable diapers for good.

At the end of that first week, I knew how to bathe the twins; I knew how to feed them; I knew how to comfort them; and I was even beginning to get some idea of how to play with them. I knew that Amit would be going back to office, and NJ would be around only in the evening, and that all day long I'd have to manage them on my own. That scared me, but I was beginning to think that maybe, just *maybe*, I could do it. This, after all, was exactly what I'd signed up for, wasn't it?

EIGHT

Settling Down

I

There was so much to be done! There was *always* so much to be done now. The work was relentless, never-ending and exhausting. All those years when I'd thought longingly of having kids of our own, I'd always thought of the fun parts – of talking to them, reading to them, teaching them things, watching them learn and play, going out with them, cooking and eating and celebrating with them. I suppose I knew there would be work to be done, I just never knew how much.

We'd always led a fairly happy-go-lucky life in the nine years we'd been married so far. Our house was cleaned on weekends, clothes were washed in the washing machine a couple of times a week, we shopped for groceries once a week or so and made everything last till the next weekend. And though we'd had a cook for the last three years, we ate whatever was readily available, even if it meant eating Maggi noodles, bread, eggs, or even cornflakes for dinner. We went out often, for a meal, or a movie, or a walk, or to meet friends. Some days, we went out in the morning and didn't return till late at night.

Suddenly, all that changed. Now I needed to organize three or four cooked meals for the kids each day. There had to be wholesome, nutritious food at home at all times – we could not afford to run out of vegetables, fruit, milk or curd at all – to say nothing of rice, dal and atta. Grocery shopping took on a whole new dimension, a life of its own. There was always something critical that we had just run out of, or that we were just about to run out of, that absolutely *had* to be procured before the next meal. And it was almost always impossible for me to run out to the nearest shop to get it, because then who would stay home with the kids? After a few weeks, I did start to do some basic grocery shopping with the kids in the stroller, but it was never easy.

What was worse was that, because we could no longer just go out for a meal whenever we found the options at home unpalatable, I also had to organize food for the two of us – and, at first, this was not the same food the kids ate. For them, I had the cook churn out bland boiled food, low in salt and spices, overcooked and mushed together. For us, this was practically indigestible, at least the thought of it was.

Then too, their mealtimes could obviously not be the same as ours; their meals would have to be closer together. This meant that it was always somebody's mealtime and there was always another meal just around the corner that I had to be prepared for.

I tried my best to deal with this new overdose of housework. I planned, I made lists, I enlisted Amit's help and I worked really hard at it – and on some days, I failed miserably. On the Wednesday after we brought the twins home, while they both napped in the afternoon, I settled down to update my blog, email distant friends and upload photos on the Net. The kids woke up before I was done. They were hungry, and I didn't have their next meal ready! It only took me half an hour or so to get it done, but getting it done with two small children hollering their heads off demanding food made me feel horribly guilty – and it gave a whole new meaning to the term 'pressure cooking'.

Food for the kids remained a tricky business for several weeks. I was never sure what would work and what wouldn't. I had no idea of what they had eaten before, what they would like and what would suit them. They both continued to have a bad digestion for several months. Their stool was unformed, stinky and occurred several times each day. Additionally, their colds were severe and still showed no signs of abating.

One day, I gave them a packaged baby cereal that had

wheat in it for breakfast. I discovered right away that wheat did not suit them. I spent the rest of that day changing dirty diapers: seventeen times in all! I also found out that diapers are no match for determined diarrhoea.

All of which notwithstanding, after the first few days, once the nausea and vomiting disappeared, our girls appeared to have a voracious appetite. Whenever they saw their food or milk bottles, they would get frantic and demand it vociferously, saying 'mam-mam-mam-mam-mam-mam' non-stop with ever-increasing volume till they got it.

'I don't think they've been getting enough to eat,' said Amit. It did look like that in those days – they ate desperately, as if afraid there wouldn't be enough food. That was sad.

'You don't have to worry,' Amit told them, 'you'll never go short of food ever again as long as you're with us.'

They were too young to understand that. But over the months, their attitude to food became more relaxed, and eventually they became secure enough to refuse food when they didn't want it.

Bathing them, initially, was something of an ordeal. Mrini hated being bathed, and if I tried to wash her hair, she screamed as if I was torturing her. This had nothing to do with having shampoo in her eyes; she just didn't like her head getting wet. This lasted for a week or so. Eventually, they came to love and enjoy their baths. Right from the beginning, I bathed them together, sitting side by side in a small, round, blue tub, and when Mrini got over her initial fear of being bathed, both of them would giggle, play and splash about in the water.

On the third day of that second week, when I was just learning to manage them on my own all day long, Tara started howling and howling right after their bath, and would not be comforted. After attempting to console her for several minutes, my patience ran out and I decided that she was simply throwing a tantrum, so I left her to howl and went away to get their lunch ready. It wasn't until many days later that I learned that children don't typically throw tantrums until they're around two years old. She must have been very hungry. I really should have given her something to nibble on while I got their lunch ready quickly, but that was just one of the many times when I simply didn't get it right.

II

The first day that Amit went to work and left me all alone with the twins – almost a week after we brought them home – I was nervous. I thought there were potentially any number of situations that I couldn't handle alone, but the worst one was the prospect of both the girls crying loudly at once. This had always been a scary thought for me, and a thought specific to adoption. It was probably an irrational belief, but I did believe that a biological mother would have no trouble understanding why her baby was crying, and no difficulty in comforting her. As an adoptive mother, I thought it would take me months to begin to understand Mrini and Tara's crying and the causes for it.

Only much later did I realize that the causes for crying are one of very few. Is she: Hungry? Thirsty? Tired? Hurt? Unwell? Frustrated? If none of these is the apparent cause, then it is unexplained. You hold her, comfort her, distract her, offer her food or water, and she'll usually be either all smiles or fast asleep in a few minutes, unless she really is unwell.

As it turned out, having two bawling and inconsolable babies on my hands never really happened to me. The few times when they did both cry together, it would be for some obvious reason, such as banging into each other and falling down. It wasn't that hard to handle.

Most things I managed to work out for myself quite soon. Apart from establishing a daily schedule, I also got them used to sleeping together – and, more importantly, falling asleep on their own – very early on, within the first three months, in fact. We continued to sleep in the same room with them until they were almost two, but they went to bed long before we did, so it was important for them to be comfortable being alone in their room in the dark and falling asleep without fear. Getting them to fall asleep on their own was so easy for us that I suspect it was a habit they had already acquired at the agency. It was a sad thought that they might, from a very early age, have been sleeping without the comfort of an adult nearby, but no sadder than a lot of other thoughts I could have had about them. At any rate, this one could be turned into a benefit for all of us.

Having two little kids around did pose certain challenges. Inevitably there were times when I couldn't be watching one or the other of them. I soon realized that making the home as child-proof as possible went a long way in reducing stress levels and frayed tempers all around. We had no beds that the twins could fall off, and no stairs. We barred access to the balconies and to the study, where we hid all the electronics as well as whatever was breakable or dangerous. Electrical appliances, which were liberally distributed throughout the house, had to be securely locked up or moved out of reach, which wasn't so easy, but eventually we got it done. The kids always discovered loopholes in our arrangements, or found ways to work around things, but for the most part, we managed to remain one step ahead.

The twins didn't appear, at first, to know what to do with toys. They didn't appear to have the concept of things to play with. Their only activity, apparently, had been playing with paper. I'd seen this happen at the agency. When they were a bit restless, a scrap of paper was given to them and they were allowed to tear it into tiny bits. Perhaps this was the only 'toy' or game the agency had funds for, but it was, to us, an unbearable habit. For almost two years, whenever the twins got their hands on any piece of paper, they could be relied upon to shred it. Since most of the papers in our home – including our vast collection of books – weren't intended for (or suitable for) shredding, it was a dangerous, exasperating habit, and one we worked hard at discouraging.

But at least they figured out the concept of toys soon enough. The first thing they learnt was the sheer joy of taking them all out of the carton they were kept in, and throwing them all over the house. Then they learnt that utensils stacked in the kitchen cupboards made very satisfactory toys and could be used to create the most amazing cacophony with very little effort. Keen to encourage them to explore, I didn't dissuade them from this, until, finally, the downstairs neighbours protested gently.

After her initial bout of adventurousness, Mrini turned out to be a shy and clingy baby, following me around, whining – and crying when Amit held her. Tara seemed to be more outgoing and cheerful, full of smiles and mischief. With time, Tara turned out to be more adventurous, while Mrini was the cautious one. Much later still, Mrini became more confident and socially outgoing, while Tara turned clingy and shy. They continued to look very much alike, so people sometimes asked me if they had similar personalities or different. Their basic personalities were always quite different, but their behaviour seemed to fluctuate, with the two of them going through cycles of behaviour that were usually perfectly out of sync with each other.

Both of them were at home in their new environment quite soon. They crawled all over the apartment and examined everything that was within their reach. They enjoyed 'going on a walk', holding one or both of my hands and having me walk all around the apartment in turns with each of them.

I was very lucky that the one milestone I did get to witness was their first step. Mrini started walking less than ten days after coming to us. She spent about forty minutes at a stretch practising very diligently to stand up, and then she decided to walk. She did a full fifteen steps before landing with a plop on her bottom. From there, there was no stopping her. She walked every day and became adept at it astonishingly quickly. I learned later that walking is something that comes gradually, with many false starts and some backtracking. For Mrini, walking came so quickly and so easily, that I wondered if perhaps she was 'over-ready' to start walking. Maybe, if she'd been given the slightest encouragement and stimulation, she would actually have started walking a few weeks earlier.

Tara started walking perhaps a month or so later, and took more time to acquire the skill. It was fascinating watching both of them learn and I was full of pride at this accomplishment of theirs – as though only our kids ever learnt to do this thing; as though I had had a key role to play in it.

Luckily also, they were still at an age where language wasn't too much of a problem. Most children start to speak around the age of one. That magical first word, contrary to television commercials, is usually some variation of 'mama'. When they came to us, the twins had, between them, a vocabulary of two words: 'akka' and 'anna' – 'sister' and 'brother' in Tamil. Presumably because their erstwhile home had been full of children of all ages, and they had heard other kids addressing older 'brothers' and 'sisters' as such, these were the words they picked up first. It was sad that they didn't make any attempt to address either of us for quite a while. When they did, 'amma' came first, and only later did they come around to 'mama'. Normally, this would have been completely unremarkable, but to the anxious ears of an adoptive mother, when 'amma' turned into 'mama' it sounded immeasurably sweeter.

Given that they must have been exposed primarily to Tamil at the agency, and that at home they were exposed to English, Hindi and Bengali in about a 70 : 20 : 10 ratio, they weren't appreciably slow in picking up language. By the time they'd been with us four months or so, each of them had a vocabulary – largely overlapping – of twenty-odd words, mostly in English. This was a relief: with the recent change in language, I'd been expecting them to speak Tamil before they learnt English or any other language known to us. In fact, they may have spoken – or at least recognized – several words in Tamil, but as we hardly knew a handful of words in Tamil, we were not the best candidates to speak it to them, or interpret any of their sounds as Tamil words. In the end, it didn't matter – they picked up English and their language skills developed roughly on par with other kids of their age.

In those early days at home, I did notice a couple of things that worried me, though. When I scolded them, Mrini put one hand on her ear, the other hand in her mouth and wore an expression of abject apology and fear. If I scolded them a little harshly, she put both hands on her ears. It was, in a way, cute, but it was also worrying. Had she frequently been punished and made to hold her ears with both hands? Had she been slapped? Or had she seen it happening to other kids? It wasn't the action itself that was worrying; it was the expression of fear that accompanied it that was.

I'd read somewhere that children who spend a lot of time in an institutional environment often have developmental delays. It was clear that our kids were small for their age, and that they might have been consistently getting less than adequate quality and quantity of nutrition in their early days. Had this had any impact on their mental development? And, if there had been any adverse impact, could it be reversed by providing good nutrition and a stable, loving environment at this stage? Could we, in any way, by any means, try to make up for their disadvantaged infancy and bring them – physically, mentally and emotionally – to a level that would be on par with their peers?

These were thoughts and questions that I had to live with for a long time, until time itself began to give us the answers.

III

After the twins had been with us for a little over four months, we had an unexpected double medical crisis on our hands. First, both of them got stomach upsets, with diarrhoea and vomiting. Mrini also had a fever. All of a sudden, early on Monday morning, she faded away before my eyes. She lay on the bed, wan and lifeless, unable to eat, unable to move, only struggling to sit up occasionally to vomit all over the bedclothes.

I phoned the doctor, who prescribed an anti-emetic and an anti-pyretic. Feeling horribly guilty, I fought to get them into her. It was no good; she couldn't keep either of them down. I tried giving her water. She drank eagerly, and a couple of moments later, that also came right back up.

That was the first time I saw either of them really

sick. They had had colds and stomach upsets pretty much through their whole time with us so far, but nothing like this.

I called Amit.

'I'll come home right away,' he said.

'Let me see how it goes, I'll let you know in an hour or so,' I told him.

An hour later, Mrini was miraculously better. Though still sick, she was smiling, playing a little and looking a lot more like her usual self. It was a complete surprise to me that a child who had appeared, less than an hour ago, to be more or less at death's door, could look so close to normal in so short a span of time.

Meanwhile, Tara, while playing with me the previous day, had managed to fall down and hit her head on the skirting of the wall. She got up shrieking, and I rushed to look at her. There was plenty of blood – I was shocked. I wiped it away and saw that there was a deep cut on her forehead.

Naturally, it had to be Sunday. We took her to the nearest doctor who was open – he ran a clinic out of his home.

'I'm not normally open on Sunday evening,' he said reluctantly when I phoned him.

I explained that blood was gushing out in large quantities (something of an exaggeration at this point; it had reduced a bit) and we didn't know where else to go (which was absolutely true), and he relented.

'Hmmmmm ... yes,' he mumbled, examining the wound a short while later. 'I don't do stitches usually,' he said, 'but if you like, I can just put one stitch here. Or you can take her to the emergency room at some nearby hospital.'

Tara, who had stopped crying by the time we got to the doctor, had started howling again now. Carting her off to the hospital, Mrini tagging along, seemed likely to only prolong the ordeal. And it was already dinner time. So, after a quick glance at each other, we agreed that he should put the stitch.

He proceeded to open his drawer and rummage around in it for a good ten minutes, while we waited. Eventually he started mumbling to himself.

'Doctor, is that what you're looking for?' I asked finally, pointing to a roll of thread on the ground.

'Of course, yes, thank you, that's it,' he said, picking it up and placing it on the table. 'Excuse me a moment.'

He came back a couple of minutes later wiping his hands on a towel. Then he cut a length of thread off the roll that had been, a moment earlier, on the ground. Then he pulled out an enormous, thick, curved needle and threaded it. Amit had already left the room, taking Mrini with him – he had no stomach for this sort of thing. I held the wailing, flailing Tara down firmly, as he pressed the edges of flesh together and pushed the needle through and knotted it. It was terrible to watch.

Then, he prescribed a preventive antibiotic for Tara, which, considering where the 'suture' had been stored, was probably just as well.

In the days that followed, it seemed like it was perpetually time for the next dose of medicine for one or the other of them. I was always thrusting medicine down one of their ungrateful gullets. I tried every trick in the book to fool them into having their medicines: giving it to them while they were standing up or lying down; disguising it with one of the more palatable tonics or supplements; and even mixing it in some favourite item of food or drink. Nothing worked. They identified the offending substance, spat it out disgustedly and ran away crying. It got so bad, that whenever they spied me approaching with something in my hand and determination on my face, they scrambled off in the opposite direction.

'They don't trust any offering from my hand right now,' I complained despairingly to my mother over the phone one day.

'I don't remember you or your sister ever behaving like that,' said my mother. 'They probably don't trust you because they are adopted.'

It was one of several thoughtless things people said that hurt me deeply.

Tara recovered soon, the way children do. We didn't even have to take her back to get the stitch cut – one day, in the morning, a week or so later, we found it lying on her bed. How she managed to take it out without tearing open the wound is a mystery, but somehow she did. The only problem was that she reacted badly to the preventive antibiotic the doctor had prescribed. By the third day, she had serious diarrhoea and vomiting, which seemed to be linked to the medicine. When I decided to stop giving it, she improved quickly. Mrini was still struggling with her stomach problem – it took almost a month for her to become completely well.

So what with Mrini's fever and Tara's stitch and antibiotic reaction, it was a difficult time for me. It wasn't the worst that could have happened; newborns, especially twins, often have to face far greater medical crises in their early days. It wasn't even the worst thing that we have had to face with the kids so far – there have been more worrying illnesses. But it was the first – and that made it a lot worse than it might otherwise have been.

IV

One of the rituals of the day, which we stuck to fairly religiously, was the evening outing to the park. We had to endure a lot of curious looks for the first several days, and I continued to be subjected to a whole lot of enquiries from the grandmotherly type for several weeks, but it was all worthwhile. Initially, the girls were very, very quiet in the park. They clung to me and wouldn't budge an inch, although they observed everything with great interest. It took months for them to start becoming more confident and outgoing in the park, but they always seemed to enjoy going. It must have been lonely for them at home, after all the noise and excitement of the orphanage.

Word got around quickly that we had adopted our kids. I fielded dozens of enquires, some politely veiled, others blunt, outright, even coarse. One particular instance stayed in my mind. There was a Punjabi matronly woman who came to the park regularly with a whole bunch of other matronly women. She took a lively interest in the twins – though even after several weeks, she couldn't tell which one was which. She and her cronies offered plenty of advice, unasked, such as:

'Feed them ragi.'
'Feed them almonds ground into milk.'
'Feed them amla paste with honey and ginger.'
'Their legs are weak. Massage them with cod liver oil.'
'Or at least with warm mustard oil.'
'Three times a day (at least).'
'Rub a mix of besan and milk on them before bathing, to lighten their complexion.'
'Give them only boiled water to drink.'
'Cover their heads and feet (or they'll catch cold).'

'Don't give them boiled water, and don't cover them up with sweaters, socks and scarves. You'll only weaken their immune systems.'

'Let them play in the sandpit.'

'Don't let them play in the sand pit (they'll only eat the sand).'

'Aren't they walking yet?'

'Aren't they talking yet?'

'Aren't they weaned from the bottle yet?'

'Aren't they toilet-trained yet?'

'Get them a walker, they'll learn to walk very soon.'

'Don't get them a walker, they'll never learn to walk.'

'My children/grandchildren learnt to walk/talk/use the toilet when he/she/they were only 3/4/5 months old.'

Most of this advice I blithely ignored, but occasionally some worry lodged in my mind and I needed a severe scolding from Amit to get rid of it.

While the twins remained very silent during the park outings, I quickly learnt that it was a good outlet for me. I made friends with other mothers and swapped stories, troubles and remedies with them. On many days, especially when Amit was travelling on work, it was my only source of adult company. It also became easier to ignore some of the dire warnings of the old biddies when you had other moms to laugh over things with.

One of my early acquaintances at the park was Sandhya,

another mother of twins. We went on to become good friends, and Mrini and Tara also became good friends with her boys. It was only after several months that she told me of a conversation that had transpired long ago between her and the old Punjabi woman.

'She asked me if I had also bought my boys from somewhere,' said Sandhya.

'What!'

'Yes, she used exactly that word, bought.'

'What does she think, they are like aloo-pyaz?' I asked, incredulous. Though she was somewhat interfering, I hadn't really thought too badly of this grandma till now.

'I don't know what she thinks,' said Sandhya with disgust. 'I asked her, "What do you mean?" She said, "No, that other woman who has twins, she bought them in Pondicherry." I just didn't know what to say.' She paused, then added, 'I didn't tell you earlier because I thought you might be hurt.'

I wasn't really hurt – just puzzled. The old woman didn't seem to be malicious, yet this was pretty nasty. It wasn't a language problem, that much was clear. And why on earth would she want to ask Sandhya this particular question? Sandhya has a porcelain complexion as do her boys – there is no doubting the parenthood in their case. To me, it seemed like a roundabout way of insulting us and the twins. And the grandma definitely knew that Sandhya and I were friends, so perhaps she knew I would hear of it. But she had always seemed so friendly…

I went out of my way to avoid that old woman and her cronies after that, and luckily, she moved out of our neighbourhood soon afterwards.

Another time, a friend was discussing some marital discord. 'I can't even walk out on him, now that we have kids,' she said to me. 'It's not so easy for us. You can just give them back, I can't do that.'

Give them back? Our daughters had been ours for over six months. They were *ours* – they had been ours from the day we took them home with us. *Give them back?* What was she talking about? It was as insensitive as telling a biological mother that she could always just abandon her baby in a ditch. Clearly my friend didn't think *that* a suitable thing to do – or say. How could she assume, that after so many months of being parents, our kids were like a piece of merchandise, to be returned whenever we wished?

She was a friend, so I made allowances. She was in a tough spot and thinking of her own troubles, her own feelings, not mine. But months later when I told Amit about this in some context, he was outraged.

'How could she say such a thing to your face?' he demanded.

'She was upset and not thinking straight,' I said.

'You don't have to be thinking straight to know that you can't say something like that,' he said. 'You shouldn't have to think at all.'

Still, I shrugged it off, convinced that she did not mean to hurt me. But it was not always so easy to avoid or ignore insensitive comments. More than once, people – friends often – told me, 'Oh, you're adopting? You're taking the easy way out. No pregnancy, no labour, it's a nice short cut to get a baby.' Others said, 'You're lucky, they are already over a year old, you won't have to get up at night, every night, to feed them.' Or, 'You'll never have to breastfeed them. That's so nice – breastfeeding is such a pain.'

Yes, that was one way of looking at it, I suppose. I could be 'lucky' to have missed out on the early days, with all the stress and exhaustion. This was a 'convenient' way to have a baby – even more so to have twins.

'But,' I said to one of these people, once, 'how can you assume that I wanted this so-called easy way out? How can you say it is "lucky" to not have given birth to your children, to know that someone else gave birth to them? How can it be a good thing to have not known your children for the whole first year of their lives? How can it be lucky to know that when they cried, you were never there to hold them – for one whole year? How can it be "nice" to not have to breastfeed them, when breastfeeding a baby is the one enduring image of motherhood in your mind? Can you honestly say that if you had been unable to have a baby – biologically – you would have been happy? Is there any part of pregnancy, delivery, or your child's infancy that you'd rather swap for the "joys" of infertility and the abandonment of your child by their biological parents?'

I probably had steam coming out of my ears at this stage – I certainly felt quite red in the face. I realized from the look on her face and her muttered backtracking that I'd overreacted. It was a pity too, because her comment had not been the first, nor the worst. She just happened to catch me at a bad time.

It's strange too; at one level, I do believe that I – we – have been lucky, incredibly lucky, to have found our girls. But it hurts to have people – especially people who know what we went through – completely dismiss the difficulties that we faced in getting here.

V

As we all settled down as a family, there were times when the demands of two small girls reduced me to tears ... and also times – times without number – when things we did to them, reduced them to tears, floods of tears and loud wails of protest too. Most times, these were routine matters: 'don't touch that,' 'don't throw that,' 'don't tear that,' 'give me that' and the like. Several times, it was medical matters; foul-tasting syrups and the regular vaccinations that all children are subject to. But the one time that was the most cruel, and which made me feel terribly guilty, was when we got their ears pierced.

Getting a daughter's ears pierced is done by almost every single family in India, so it was far from being a unique experience. Our problem was that we'd left it so late. For many months, we hadn't the heart to put the twins – and ourselves – through it, so when we finally decided that we had to do this, they were close to two-and-a-half years old. Naturally, it was a traumatic experience for all of us. My parents had never had my ears pierced as a child. I finally got it done just before my wedding, when I was all of twenty-four years old. I still remember how much it hurt. It could hardly have been any less for a two-year-old, and it would certainly have been quite incomprehensible to them that we, their trusted parents, were putting them through this.

They were both still crying loudly as we walked away from the jeweller's shop. To distract them – and perhaps also in an attempt to assuage our own consciences – we decided to walk to a nearby toy shop, where they could explore some of the varied goods on offer and we could spend some money on them. As we were walking past a row of houses on the way, a voice called from the terrace of one house. 'Hey! Whose children are you walking away with?'

It was the first – but not the last – time that we were publicly accused of kidnapping our kids. I was shocked speechless. Amit, with greater presence of mind, shouted back, 'What's it to you?' and followed it up with some choice abuses. 'If he'd been down here, I'd have hit him,' he said to me.

The kids had been ours for well over a year by this time. I'd stopped thinking of them as 'adopted'. They were just our kids. Our behaviour with each other was just the same as any other family; only our features and complexions were different. It no longer occurred to me that people looking at us would see us as anything other than a family. And yet, all it took was for both girls to be crying audibly as we walked down a road.

The second time a similar thing happened was at a crowded railway station late at night several months later. That time, it was completely uncalled for. The girls were walking along quietly, tired but not crying or unhappy in any visible way. Still, a hanger-on shouted after us. This time, Amit really did run after the lout and almost hit him. This time though, it was easier for me to shrug it off. Such things would happen ... and perhaps there were worse comments and insinuations in store for us in the future. Right now, thankfully, the girls were still too young to understand such comments; soon, they wouldn't be. And there would always be these insensitive (or well-meaning?) interfering people around to say things. We would all just have to acquire a thick skin and get past them.

Sometimes, it was a simple and innocuous comment,

made in good faith. A friend once said their eyes were just like mine. It took several moments for her to realize the futility of that compliment. When they turned five, their paediatrician remarked on their height – from being in the bottom five percentile, they had shot up to above average. 'They take after you,' she said, nodding at Amit. Then, immediately realizing her mistake, she went red with embarrassment. Several months later, a woman in the locker room of our gym eyed the girls for a few minutes and then said, 'They don't look like you.' She was discomfited when I told her, in an offhand way, 'Oh, they're adopted.' She hadn't even thought of that.

These incidents – and many more like these – did not hurt. It was not hurtful to simply acknowledge the fact of their adoption, the fact of their physical differences from Amit and me. It irritated me when people assumed our family unit to be somehow inferior, somehow less than whole or less than healthy because of adoption, but I learnt to acquire a thick skin on that subject too. Still, sometimes my own insecurity as an adoptive mother was exposed – not so much by people outside the family as by our family itself.

The twins had been with us for about six months, when I had to make a quick trip to Pondicherry as part of the legal process of filing for adoption. We planned it so that I left Bangalore at night, after they were asleep, and returned the next evening, before they went to sleep. 'Only twenty-four hours away from them,' I said to Amit. 'I think we can all handle it.'

'In any case, this is the only way,' he said. 'I have an important meeting, I can't go. And we can't delay this any more.'

At that stage, I still hadn't read enough parenting books to know that you need to talk to your kids, even if you think they won't understand. So I didn't say a word to them about my being away for one whole day. They were, after all, only one-and-a-half years old.

While I was away, Amit held fort admirably. The kids were their usual selves. There were only a couple of minor crises along the lines of 'where is the...' and 'whose is this?' I returned the next evening eager to greet my babies and hold them and hug them. So I was shocked when Mrini saw me and ran in the opposite direction. Mrini! My darling, clingy mommy's girl!

I greeted Tara first and she was happy and cheerful and entirely unperturbed. Then I went after Mrini. But she was having none of it. She cried when I went near her, and headed determinedly for any room that didn't have me in it. If Amit went to her, she was happy, but she didn't want anything to do with me. She kept it up the entire evening, and only the next day did she snap back to her usual sunny self. Unprepared as I was for such a reception, I was upset that day and for several days after that. Had they still not accepted me as their mother? Was it still such a fragile bond? I felt guilty for having gone away, but I had come back as quickly as humanly possible and it was something that just had to be done. Did it merit this kind of punishment?

It might have been the same if a biological mother who spent her entire day with her kids had to suddenly go away for one whole day. But a biological mother would have shrugged it off without a second thought. She, I felt, would not have worried about her bond with her child. That bond was unquestioned, unquestionable – by oneself and by others.

And that was the burden I carried as an adoptive mother – the burden of my own insecurity. At so many stages, in so many instances, I questioned myself and my ability as a mother. I wondered if I was in some indefinable way inferior to other mothers, just by virtue of being an adoptive mother. Did I – adoptive mother that I was – measure up? In those early days, I didn't know for sure. That was why I remained vulnerable to jibes from strangers and friends.

One thing I was sure of. I didn't hold the fact of their adoption against them – in my heart, I did not and I knew that with certainty. But did they, somehow, in their hearts, in that deep, underground place where no words are formed, did they hold the fact of their adoption against me?

VI

We never had a large, grand homecoming party for our babies. Though the idea was appealing, I had read that it was usually unsettling for the child and that made sense. So we introduced them to our friends and family in ones and twos. First to arrive was Sridhar, who came with a vast armload of diapers. He promptly earned the sobriquet of 'diaper-uncle', which, luckily, did not endure for too long. The twins took to him right away, and one of the earliest photographs we have of them is of them being held by Sridhar.

Later, in the weeks that followed, other friends came by in ones and twos. We were surprised when, occasionally, people we didn't know very well just dropped in, or sometimes expressed an interest in being invited to meet the twins. One of our neighbours left a note at our door: 'Would like to meet you, please let me know a convenient time.'

We communicated a convenient time, and he came over one evening.

'I heard you adopted these girls,' he said right away.

'Yes,' I said, smiling. We had apparently created quite a sensation in our apartment complex by appearing one day with two one-year-olds.

'What is the process like,' he enquired, engaging Tara in play. 'Actually, my brother and sister-in-law are unable to have a child. They want to adopt, but they are not very sure about it.'

We explained how it had been for us, and after an hour or so, he left. I greeted his wife often after that, and she often chatted with the kids. It was almost two years later when she told me, one day, that her husband's brother and sister-in-law had just adopted a baby girl. 'She is three months old and they got her just last week,' she said, and added, 'They were partly inspired by hearing about you. They had been considering adoption, but when my husband spoke to them about you and your family, they felt encouraged to make up their minds.'

When people got to know that we had adopted, many of them would ask me about adoption. A common question was, 'What about your parents and in-laws? Was there any opposition?'

In our family, there was no opposition to us adopting our children. In Amit's family, ours is not the only childless marriage; while in my family, the number of first cousins I have on either side of the family is incredibly small. So in both cases, additions to the family, even in a 'non-traditional' way, were more than welcome. Even if anyone had been against adoption 'in principle', I doubt that would have swayed our decision. Whether or not to adopt, for us, in our nuclear family, was very much our decision, no one else's.

Amit's father was the first family member to come and

visit us after the adoption. After him, my sister visited, and then my parents. By December of that year, three short months since their homecoming, we were ready to visit Kolkata, and show off our babies to Amit's extended family. There, for the first time, a huge party was arranged for everyone to come and meet the twins. The twins held up fairly well though, and smiled through most of it, as they were passed around from lap to lap like an involved game of passing the parcel. If they were at all unsettled by the trip away from home, by the change of food, environment, climate and family, they didn't show it too much. They were a little more clingy and cranky than usual by the end of the trip, but nothing worse than that.

'I wonder if they think this is their new home,' I said to Amit while we were in Kolkata. 'I hope they don't think they've been uprooted from their home again.' It was a fear that haunted me in different ways for several months. So it was very reassuring to see, when we finally got back home, the twins' eyes light up. Tired as they were from the flight, they ran to their room and greeted their old toys with squeals of joy. They knew they were home now.

Although most of our friends came and met our twins in ones and twos over the months, we didn't have any kind of homecoming party for them until June the following year. It wasn't that they couldn't have managed it earlier; it was more that *we* weren't ready for it until then. It was ironic that it was almost nine months to the day after the twins' homecoming – like an inside out pregnancy period. When it happened, our party was neither huge nor grand; it was instead a homely affair to which our closest friends, about ten-odd families, were invited, and for which I cooked all the food myself at home, while Amit set things up and managed the girls.

It was so good to see all our friends gather there that evening – friends I'd hardly been able to look in the eye at one point. There were Sridhar and Sowmya, with their baby, Jathi, just a few months old now; Vyom and Vipra, with Vidit, now almost two, just a few weeks older than our twins; Arvind and Priya, with their little girl; Arvind and Soma, expecting their second; Manasi, of course, without whose help I would never have survived those first few days, along with her husband Sachin, and their daughter Aabha; all of them and others, laughing, talking, drinking, cheering – all celebrating our own two little miracles.

At the end of that day, as we looked back over the party itself, and then over all that it marked, all that we had celebrated, we felt blessed. People have told us, time and again, that we would be blessed for the 'noble' deed of adopting two orphan children, that the children were so 'lucky' to have been adopted by us. Time and again, I replied: No, *we* are the lucky ones. We have been blessed.

NINE

The Paperwork: GAWA

I

We might have hoped that once we had brought our girls home and all of us had settled down to life together as a family, the matter of 'adoption' was over. We might have thought that now we could all just get on with our lives. But there was still the little matter of the legalities of adoption, the paperwork.

At the agency, when we first met the kids and the whole process of adoption began to seem immediate and real, we were told that we'd have to visit Pondicherry at least five or six times over the next year to complete the legalities related to the adoption. I vaguely wondered how we would manage it, and I looked at Amit enquiringly, but at that time, we just nodded blankly. There was too much happening in each moment to seriously worry about anything that far away. We didn't know then that Pondicherry would be a constant companion in our busy lives over the next three years; that we'd visit so often that our regular hotel would start giving us 'frequent visitor' discounts, unasked for, before the legal process was through; that we'd end up exploring every means of transport between Bangalore and Pondicherry other than walking, in the hope of finding one that was a little less uncomfortable for our two growing, squirming, active kids.

It wasn't, it seemed, anything specific to our case that caused the adoption legalities to be so long drawn out and so tiresome. We just happened to have found our babies in Pondicherry, which must be one of the most difficult states in India to adopt a child from. The tenacity, fortitude and perseverance required to complete adoption legalities from Pondicherry completely defy description. If we'd had to go through this process for anything other than our two daughters, we would certainly have given up halfway.

In addition to the normal nuances of the legal system, our case was compounded by the complications involved in an out-of-state adoption. This meant that every interaction with the lawyer, with the court, or with anyone else meant making a trip out of town – 300 km or so each way, which involved a seven-hour drive. On most of these trips, the children were not required; but as we had no one to leave them with, we always had to take them along, effectively turning each quick trip into a major expedition.

Hindus in India must adopt a child under the Hindu Adoption and Maintenance Act (HAMA) of 1956. For people of other faiths, or for citizens of other countries who adopt from India, the Guardians and Wards Act (GAWA) of 1890 is applicable. (Nowadays the Juvenile Justice Act of 2006 is also used for adoption, but it was not applicable in our case.) Under GAWA, adoptive parents get custody of an adopted child, and are appointed legal guardians of the child; but only under HAMA do adoptive parents legally become parents of the adopted child.

The crucial difference between the two Acts is that of succession. Under HAMA, an adopted child is heir to the parents' estate and is considered equivalent to a biological child. Under GAWA, the parents' responsibility for the child legally ends when the child turns eighteen; and children adopted under GAWA do not automatically inherit their adoptive parents' estate when the parents pass away. Parents must specifically will their estate to children adopted under GAWA; if they die without a will, their estate will be subject to the laws of succession.

There is another worrying difference between GAWA and HAMA that we didn't find out about until our lawyer told us much later: under GAWA, the guardianship awarded to you could be revoked by the court at any time. I suppose there would have to be solid grounds for doing so, and perhaps it doesn't usually happen, but it created a niggling little fear in us all the same. GAWA was not final and irrevocable; for that we would have to go through HAMA.

Being Hindu by birth (and leaving personal convictions out of this discussion), Amit and I would normally be expected to adopt under HAMA anyway. In most states, so I heard many times and from many sources, adoption under HAMA takes a few months and requires parents and adopted child to appear in court only once. But in Pondicherry alone, due to its being a Union territory and having been under French rule till relatively recently (de facto 1954; de jure 1962), the adoption laws were slightly different.

First, we had to keep our children under 'foster care' for a minimum period of three months. This is to ensure that the adopted child settles down in the new family environment and that the family also achieves a level of comfort with the child.

After at least three months, we could file for adoption under GAWA. This appeal would be filed in the family court in Pondicherry. 'You have to appear in person for each hearing,' said our lawyer. 'Unlike in the civil court, I cannot actually represent you in the family court. I can only appear as amicus curae. Both petitioners have to appear in person each time.'

So one hot April afternoon, all of us piled into a rental car and started on the long drive to Pondicherry. The twins, who were about one-and-a-half by now, slept for part of the journey, and were happy enough playing in our laps the rest of the time. It was rare for them to have our undivided attention for such a long span of time, and they were quite happy about it. By the time we reached Pondicherry, around midnight, they were asleep again, but they woke up when we got out and went up to our room, and stayed awake until we turned out the lights an hour or so later.

The next morning, we rushed to get ready by 8 a.m. and reached the lawyer's office at 9 a.m. We were made to hurriedly sign a bunch of papers that we hardly got a chance to glance at, and then we left for the family court. This was in a small, crumbling building on a corner of Goubert Avenue, looking straight out at the dull grey sea. Pondicherry, unfortunately, does not have a beach here – only a broad pavement running along the road, called the Promenade, and an ugly stretch of big, black rocks keeping the sea at bay. Although it's a long, straight road and the restless sea should make it attractive and breezy, it is also humid, stifling, sunny and practically devoid of shade.

We weren't there for sightseeing, but as it turned out, we spent a lot of time gazing at the restless grey sea and the long, hot Promenade as we waited for the judge to arrive and for our case to be called.

Filing papers was usually the first order of business, we were told, and in fact we were called at 10.15 a.m. after waiting just a few minutes. Amit pushed his way through the throng of waiting people to the front of the hall, and I followed behind, each of us holding one of the children. By the time he had reached the front, our case was done and the next case was called.

'So why did we have to come all the way for this,' I asked Amit irately. 'Any passer-by would have done just as well, for all the attention he paid to any of us.'

Our lawyer came sweeping out. 'Wait here,' she mumbled sternly, and vanished through the throng.

We waited another two hours. Two hours of waiting with two small kids in the midst of a milling crowd of sweating bodies in an airless passageway is sheer torture – even if you do have a view of the sea a stone's throw away. One after the other, both kids had a mini meltdown. Eventually, I decided to take them both out of the building, and leave Amit to wait for the lawyer and find out what to do next. 'Call me on my mobile and I'll come straight up if you need me,' I said. The use of mobile phones was not allowed inside the courthouse, but I didn't see any option at this point.

I took the kids down to the sandy pavement and let them play there for a while. The sun was fierce and Tara started to cry unstoppably after some time. Mrini added her voice just for good measure, and I was at the end of my wits. I had just managed to walk them to a small snack shop and give them some cool water when Amit emerged from the building.

'Apparently we had to wait for the case to be numbered,' he said. 'I was given a date for when we will know about the first hearing.'

'Oh, do we have a date for the first hearing, already?' I asked, confused.

'No, we have a date for when we will *get* the date for the first hearing,' said Amit. 'I had to sign some things and the case will have to be numbered in the next few days.'

And we three had been made to wait two extra hours for *that*?

II

We went straight back to the hotel, where, after cooling down and drinking lots of water, both the kids eventually recovered their composure. After a quick lunch, we were back in the car and back on the road to Bangalore. While Amit and the kids slept, I read the papers that we had signed that morning. That was when I noticed where it said that I was currently employed as a technical writer with such-and-such a company, earning so much per month, and therefore financially capable of managing the kids. I noticed it, in a sleep-deprived sort of way, and thought nothing of it. It wasn't until the next day that the penny quietly dropped in my mind.

Hang on, I *wasn't* currently employed. I'd quit my job more than six months ago! *What* was the date on this document? April 2008? That wasn't right. Would we have to do something about that? Surely it wouldn't do to make that kind of a mistake in a legal document we were filing in a court?

We pointed out to the lawyer that I wasn't currently employed. 'Why didn't you say so that morning, when you came to sign the papers?' she asked in an irritated tone. With the greatest tact, Amit forebore to retort that we'd hardly had time to sign the papers, let alone read them that morning. 'What can we do to correct it, now?' he asked politely.

'It may not have been numbered yet,' she said brusquely. 'I'll ask the court clerk not to number it now. It is easy to make a change before it is numbered, after that it is a more complicated process. Either one of you can come down to withdraw the papers, make the change and resubmit it to the court. But you have to come within a month of the date of submission.'

Just over a month later, I was back in Pondicherry. This time, I was alone – which made it all much easier. Since I was travelling alone, I took the overnight bus to Pondicherry, and was at the bus stand at the ungodly hour of 4.30 a.m. At 7.30 a.m., I started walking, and after taking a highly convoluted and roundabout route, and getting lost a few times, I reached the courthouse at 8.30 a.m.

(It shouldn't have taken more than twenty minutes, as I discovered later.) I called the lawyer, who said she would come by 9.30. She finally turned up at 9.45, shortly *after* the judge had arrived. She succeeded in locating our case papers and getting the clerk to return them to us, but there was no time to actually make the changes before the judge was seated at ten. I was rushed into the courtroom, my papers were passed up to the judge, he called Amit's name, looked up and saw me, nodded, passed the papers back down and then I was ushered out of the courtroom. After waiting a few minutes, our papers returned to the court clerk in the back room, and it was now that the lawyer set about making the requisite corrections. I signed half a dozen times, and by 10.30 it was all done. Now the case could be numbered, and after that a date for the first hearing would be set. It would be in about a month from now.

'Do we both have to come for the hearing?' I asked the lawyer again. I knew the answer already, but I was still hoping she'd find a way so that either one of us could come, then we wouldn't have to drag the kids all the way to Pondicherry multiple times.

'Yes, you both have to come,' she said.

'Amit might be travelling around that time,' I said. 'If he is going to be out of town on that date, can we request another date?'

'No, whatever date is given, you have to come on that date,' said the lawyer coldly.

This was quite worrying, because Amit often had official trips that were planned well in advance and it would be difficult for him to get out of one of those; but as it turned out, the dates did not clash.

III

The first hearing was set for Friday the thirteenth. Luckily, we aren't the superstitious kind, and anyway, we had other things to worry about.

'What time will it be?' Amit asked the lawyer over the telephone.

'I can't tell you the time. You have to be in court from 10 a.m. to 6 p.m. You can be called at any time. There'll be a lunch break for an hour.'

We'd had the kids for almost nine months now and one thing I could say for sure: they weren't such quiet, timid, placid little babies any more. They were almost two years old and they needed attention, they needed stimulation, they needed regular food at mealtimes and space to lie down at nap times. And they needed diaper changes, of course.

'Actually, we will have the kids with us, so can my wife wait at the hotel with the kids and come to the court just a short while before our case is called?' asked Amit.

'No, your case can be called at any time,' she repeated

with some irritation. 'You don't have to bring the kids, you can leave them with someone.'

Easier said than done. It's not easy handling two toddlers for a couple of days, and when they are not your own two toddlers, it's something anyone would be well advised to steer clear of.

'Maybe we can ask your sister to come to Pondicherry with us,' Amit suggested. 'She can be at the hotel with the kids while we are in court.'

It looked like our only option. My sister, Anjali, lived in Delhi and was only slightly acquainted with the twins, but she was young and sensible and she might be able to manage. On the other hand though, Mrini and Tara were a handful. They tended to get into all sorts of trouble when confined in a hotel room. We had spent a good part of our previous stay just telling them things like 'don't play with that light switch', 'keep your hands out of the mini bar' and 'don't throw your toys at the TV'. We also had to fend a few call-backs from room service, whom they succeeded in dialling on the phone. So my dear sister would certainly not have an easy time of it, quite apart from feeding them lunch, changing their diapers and putting them to bed.

'Let's talk to someone about this,' I said.

I phoned around and got in touch with a lawyer in Bangalore who also worked on adoption cases. He was very helpful and – more importantly – very reassuring. First, he confirmed one aspect of our case that had been worrying us, and which our own lawyer had not properly clarified: In Pondicherry, and only in Pondicherry, we would indeed have to go through both GAWA and HAMA serially. In the rest of India, adoption is done under either one.

'How about the date of the hearing?' I asked him. 'If Amit is travelling, can we somehow request a change of date?'

'Of course you can,' he said confidently. 'It might be better if you can attend on the given date, but if you absolutely cannot, you can ask for another date.'

I then outlined my concern about keeping the kids in court the whole day. 'Is it really so stringent that if I take them out for a few minutes, to the bathroom or something, and right at that time our case is called, and if I am not there, the hearing will not happen?'

He almost laughed then. 'There is usually a list put up outside the court in the morning, which lists the order of the cases to be called for that day. It might be in Tamil, you can ask your lawyer to check it and tell you. Then you can ask your husband to wait at the court and to call you when there are two or three cases ahead of yours,' he said. 'In any case, first hearings are usually in the morning, right after submission of new cases.'

Based on this information, we decided we'd try to manage this trip without roping in my sister or anyone else. In the end, it wasn't too bad. We hired a car and were driven down on Thursday afternoon. Apart from some inevitable carsickness, it was an uneventful drive, though we arrived at Pondicherry rather late and it was past midnight by the time we all fell asleep.

The next morning, we all went to the courthouse together to check the schedule for the day. The good news was that the court clerk told us ours would be the first case that morning. The bad news was that there was no sign of our lawyer, even at 10.15 a.m. when the judge was in court and some preliminary business was being completed. She finally came up the steps in a leisurely manner and swept past us and into the courtroom in stony silence. Five minutes later, our case was called, and all four of us found our way to the front of the courtroom. A brief exchange took place between the lawyer and the judge (in Tamil), and we were told to come for the next hearing two weeks later.

And that was that. Our thirty seconds in the spotlight were over before we had quite realized they had begun.

What was supposed to have happened was that the Department for Social Welfare was supposed to have said that they had no objection to us adopting the twins. What in fact happened is anyone's guess. Amit says he signed something again, but he had no clue what it was. The judge hardly glanced at us or at our papers. Still, apparently something *had* happened, and we were to appear for a similar 'something' two weeks later.

IV

It was much the same thing two weeks later when we were back in court. This time, Amit actually got to stand in a box and hold his hand out and say, 'I swear to tell the truth.' The judge flipped through our papers and spoke to the lawyer and the court clerk. Other unrelated lawyers were laughing and talking in whispers amongst themselves, like backbenchers in college. Mrini and Tara, who were entertaining some of the audience in this scene, caused a minor diversion by starting to scream softly. Then we were all quickly hustled out of the courtroom.

Apparently, we were all done. 'The judge has passed the order,' our lawyer told us urgently. We were lucky – sometimes, it took yet another hearing (or two) for this to happen. 'It will take a month or so for the order to come,' continued the lawyer. 'Once it comes, we can apply for the birth certificate and also file for adoption in the civil court under HAMA.'

That sounded simple. But that evening, while I kept the kids entertained at the hotel, Amit went and spoke to the lawyer at length. That conversation changed things. Somewhere in that conversation, she changed from being a sort of stony adversary to being a person who was actually trying to help us.

In subsequent conversations over the next several hearings and many months she almost became a friend.

Amit was the one who handled all the interactions with her, but on the rare occasions that I was present, I even saw her actually smiling.

'She says she's doing these adoption cases out of a genuine interest to help these kids in their new homes. She's not doing it for the money,' Amit told me. That much, at any rate, seemed believable – her fees were very reasonable. 'And by the way, we're going to be coming to Pondicherry several times, so don't think we're done here yet.'

'Surely just one more trip, for HAMA?' I asked.

'First, we wait for the order to come. Once that comes, we have to come here to get the adoption deed registered. For that, we have to go to the registrar's office along with the girls. We also have to get an X-ray done on them to determine their age.'

'But we know their age, we know their exact date and time of birth. It's on the hospital's record and the agency has it,' I protested.

'I know that, but apparently we still have to get it done,' said Amit patiently. 'It can be done on the same trip when we come to get the adoption deed registered.'

'Can't we get it done in Bangalore?' I asked. 'The X-ray business, I mean.'

'I suggested it, but the lawyer said that the report has to go to the chief medical officer, so it's easy if we do it here, she will pick it up and send it to the CMO directly.'

'Okay, so all of that is one trip. What next?'

'Then we have to be interviewed by the sub-divisional magistrate,' said Amit. That sounded exciting. 'All four of us,' he added. 'And she also said that sometimes he can ask quite a few questions, more than the judge. And, what's more, this meeting with the sub-divisional magistrate can be a chancey affair. Sometimes it gets cancelled at the last minute, or pushed out by a day or two. So we have to be prepared for a couple of extra days for that one.'

Very exciting indeed, with two little kids in tow.

'And *after* that, there's HAMA,' concluded Amit.

We certainly had a long way to go. And, what's worse, we left Pondicherry the next morning without even the one piece of paper we had come to get – the court order giving us legal guardianship of the twins. Even that would take another month.

V

It was two months before we returned to Pondicherry for the registration of the adoption deed and the x-ray for age determination. It was a difficult and exhausting trip. We started the drive early in the morning, for a change, to avoid the late-night sleep disruption. We met the lawyer post-lunch, at around 2 p.m. There was a group of about six families all heading for the registrar's office to get their adoption deeds registered. In a way it was good, because the various children could watch each other and even try to socialize. But more than a couple of hours hanging around in a sweaty, stuffy office with two toddlers who've spent the morning cooped up in a car is bound to end in crisis. Both girls became cranky. They wanted water and they wanted to sleep and they wanted to get out of there.

Well after we were all tired past endurance, we were called. Digital photographs were taken and thumb impressions were scanned. Just as it seemed we might actually finish here, Tara tugged on a dangling network cable and everything came to a grinding halt. It took them forever to figure out what exactly had caused the network connection to fail, to fix it, to get back online again and to redo whatever they had been doing when they lost the connection. It was close to 6 p.m. when we finally got out of there.

Now we had to go for the X-ray. Though the X-ray itself was simple enough – both wrists and both knees of each girl – it was another long haul at the end of a long day. There was the usual long wait, the girls' usual restiveness, the technician's usual tardiness. It was past 8.30 by the time we got back to the hotel and ordered dinner. As usual, we were too tired to celebrate yet another successful trip. Besides, we knew we'd be coming back sooner or later.

For the next six months or so, we stayed away from Pondicherry. Then, all of a sudden, we were called for the meeting with the sub-divisional magistrate, or SDM as he was referred to. We got the call on a Monday night, and were told to be there by 9 a.m. on Wednesday morning, so it was a bit of a rush. Somehow we left the next day and reached Pondicherry late at night – again.

The next day we were at the lawyer's office at 9 a.m. sharp, bathed, fed and generally rested. There were six or seven other families there too, mostly the same families we had encountered the last time. The lawyer put each family through their paces by asking a set of questions which she expected the SDM might possibly ask. We all left her office in a mini convoy at 9.55 and were at the SDM's court by 10.05.

For the next two hours, we all hung around, waiting, trying to keep eight young kids under control. Luckily, there was nobody else in the court, so the kids had a certain degree of freedom. Some of them went and played in the witness box, until something happened that resulted in a crash and loud wailing from two of the witnesses, after which the witness stand remained vacant. So did the judge's chair, however; we were told the SDM was in a meeting, which might end around 11.30, and that he would then have to go into another meeting at noon. So he would, maybe, squeeze us in in the half-hour between meetings.

At 11.45 or so, we were urgently shepherded into another, smaller room, which had a large desk, a smaller computer table close to it and at right angles to it, windows, a door (apparently to a private toilet) and a huge number of chairs. It was a smaller room, but by no means a small room. The SDM was a youngish chap who was in a big hurry and quite curt with his staff, who were busying themselves around him. He grabbed a sheaf of papers and called a name: Nayantara Mukherjee. Amit and I swarmed to the front of the room with both kids, Amit saying as he went that they were twins.

'Date of birth?' enquired the SDM brusquely.

'The 25th of August, 2006,' replied Amit.

The SDM frowned and then said, 'Are you sure it isn't April?'

Amit kept his composure (which is more than I would have done) and affirmed that it was not April, but, in fact, August.

'Then this date is wrong,' barked the SDM, holding out a sheet of paper to one of his assistants.

The hapless assistant took it from him, glanced at the name and called another child. Tara's turn, apparently, was over. Before we could blink, the other child's turn was over as well, and the SDM had delegated the rest of the work to one of his staff members and left the room.

How about poor Mrinalinee Mukherjee?

Two of the staff members laboriously went through the rest of the papers, calling each child in turn, checking dates of birth, initialling something, and going on to the next. Mrini was almost the last to be called. By this time, it was just past noon, and we were all shooed out of the room, out of the building and asked to wait some more, while they checked some part of the formalities with someone on the phone. After fifteen minutes, we were given the all-clear: we could go.

As we made our long, tiring way home, we consoled ourselves with the thought that a two-hour wait in a government office to successfully accomplish something is pretty good going, really. We didn't have to make multiple trips, or even stay an extra day. And, what's more, apart from general restlessness during the long car journey, the kids were pretty well behaved and didn't cause us too much tension.

And it was slowly beginning to seem as though we were gradually getting to the end of our innumerable, interminable trips to Pondicherry. 'Just one more trip ... only one more and then we're done,' we told each other consolingly, as the kids sprawled in an ungainly fashion all over the back seat of the car and tried to sleep. They were getting too big for this.

VI

In March 2009, a year and a half after our daughters came home, we finally got their birth certificates. At last, we had a document where we were named as their parents. It was a formality, a legality, but an important one. Maybe it shouldn't have mattered, but it did. Here, at last, was a formal, significant, somehow *meaningful* document naming us as the parents of Mrinalinee Mukherjee and Nayantara Mukherjee. Perhaps as much to reassure ourselves as for any other reason, we had requested twenty copies of each birth certificate. When we finally got them, we were so happy that at first we didn't even notice the minor errors in names and addresses. A long process of return and correction followed, but it wasn't important. The main thing was that we had finally got their birth certificates.

TEN

The Paperwork: HAMA

I

In December 2009, our lawyer told us we should file for adoption under HAMA in the civil court. Why the long wait? She had advised us to wait for the long backlog of cases to be cleared. Now was a good time, she said. But in order to file the petition in the civil court, we'd have to first go to the family court and get our papers returned to us.

'Earlier only one petitioner was required,' she explained to Amit, 'but now they've changed the rules and both petitioners have to be present.'

Why did they always change the rules just as our turn came up? Why couldn't they have changed them just a little bit later? Wearily, we picked a date – a luxury, when the date was usually decided for us by the court – and prepared ourselves for the long drive down to Pondicherry yet again.

'Let's drive this time,' said Amit. 'It's a really tight squeeze in the back of a taxi.'

'Yes, it is. But then, keeping the kids tied up in their car seats for seven hours is just criminal,' I countered. 'They'll be so bored and restless.'

'It's not any too easy keeping them occupied with the four of us crammed into the back of an Indica,' said Amit. 'Plus, you know, there are the long delays at the borders where the taxi will be stopped for tax.'

After debating the matter some more, we decided to take a train to Chennai, and then go by road from there to Pondicherry. 'At least the train journey will be easy,' said Amit. 'There's a toilet on the train and the kids can move around a bit. And the drive from Chennai to Pondicherry only takes about three hours, it's not that long. We can even take a local bus. The kids should experience a bit of that as well, instead of getting used to the luxury of an air-conditioned car all the time.'

In the end, it was the toilet argument that convinced me, so we booked tickets on the early morning train to Chennai. The train journey was not too bad, apart from the small inconvenience of having to get out of bed at 4.30 a.m. to board the train at 6.00 a.m. We reached Chennai mid-morning, hopped on a bus to the bus stand and, by noon, were on a bus headed to Pondicherry.

What a bus it was! If we wanted to give the kids a flavour of travelling by local transport, we couldn't have chosen a better way to do it. We were squeezed into a tiny space right at the back of the bus and, even so, had a constant stream of humanity falling over us. The bus rattled on at snail's pace and the heat was insufferable. And just when it seemed that the end was not too far off, we stopped for lunch! I had wanted to spare the children the discomfort of being strapped into car seats for seven hours, only to have them sandwiched between us in an equally immobile position for close to five hours. At last we reached Pondicherry around 4.00 p.m. – a good twelve hours after we'd left home.

The next day was the usual run-around. We went to the lawyer's house, then to the court. It was in a new building now, a spanking new, gleaming white, imperial building, spacious, graceful and with a small patch of green lawn in the central courtyard. That green lawn was our saviour. For the long hours we spent hanging around the courthouse, it was the green lawn that was home to the twins and me, while Amit and the lawyer paced the corridor outside the court room.

At first, things didn't go too well. Four lawyers and a judge had passed away that weekend, so courts were closed and judges were away paying condolences to the bereaved. Our lawyer, however, was not put out by such matters. She persuaded the court clerk to persuade the judge to hear our case in his chambers, which he did. He was also informed that we had travelled to Pondicherry all the way from Bangalore just for this work, so would he kindly pass the order the same day? To our relief, he agreed! But there was a catch, of course: he had a doctor's appointment at 4 p.m. He would come back to court after that, and we would have our order then.

So at 4 p.m., with sleepy kids in tow, we were back at the courthouse. I had many misgivings – how many people, after a doctor's appointment at 4 p.m., would return to work for just the little while that remained? Luckily, our judge did not think in my irresponsible fashion, and at 4.45 p.m., he was back and our order was passed. We rushed to the records section and waited another half-hour while our papers were located and 'returned' – straight into our lawyer's hands. We both had to sign something. This was the only two seconds for which I was required – this utterly insignificant signature was the entire reason for which the kids and I had had to endure this long, hot, tiring, frustrating, roller-coaster journey.

The return journey was almost as difficult and tiring as the outward journey had been. And yet, we told ourselves again, it was all worthwhile. 'We are one step closer to the end,' we consoled each other. The lawyer would file the petition for HAMA in the civil court. There would normally be only one hearing for which all four of us would be required; at other hearings, if any, she would represent us.

'This time, we *really* are closer to the end of this long road,' said Amit. But you just never know.

II

Our first HAMA hearing was scheduled for 9 February 2010. 'You don't have to come for that,' the lawyer told Amit. 'You will be required for the next hearing, and the case will be closed within sixty days of this hearing.'

So things were looking better: now we had a date for the end of this long procedure.

'But before this hearing on 9 February, someone from the Indian Council for Social Welfare will come to meet you,' the lawyer added.

'Meet us? Okay,' said Amit.

'He will see your residence, and he will ask you some questions about the adoption and about your family life,' said the lawyer.

'What kind of questions?' asked Amit.

'He will ask a lot of general questions,' said the lawyer, 'but he can also ask some awkward questions. Like, he might say, "Why are your daughters so dark, don't you bathe them?" or he might say, "They are too thin. You are not feeding them enough." He is known to be a slightly tricky person, so just stay cool, answer to the point, don't say anything extra and don't get upset by anything he says,' she cautioned us. 'And if he says anything about your infertility, just ignore it. There is a court ruling that infertility and its causes cannot be questioned in court, so you don't have to give any explanations or any more documents about it.'

It was just as well to be forewarned.

Dr S contacted us and said he would meet us on Saturday, 6 February. 'I will come maybe around twelve or so. Sometime around lunchtime,' he told Amit on the phone.

'Lunchtime? Do I have to offer him lunch?' I asked Amit.

'No – not if he's going to ask nasty questions,' Amit replied. 'Just make him some foul tea and let's send him away as quickly as possible.'

Meanwhile, on Friday evening, we had to rush around to the kids' doctor – Dr S wanted a medical certificate stating that they were in good health. He also wanted a doctor's certificate testifying to visible identification marks. Luckily, the doctor who had sewed up Tara's forehead was in the next building and he had seen the twins often enough. We asked him for these certificates and, somewhat reluctantly, he agreed to put something on paper. Dr S also wanted a general clean bill of health for the two of us, but our local doctor flatly refused to give any such certificate without running some blood tests first.

'Look, do we really have to do this?' I asked Amit in

frustration. We've already given a full medical test and been certified medically fit to adopt back when we registered for adoption. Even if we have contracted some deadly disease now, are they going to take the children away from us?' That would be ... inconceivable. Nobody would do that for parents who had their children the normal way. Why should we have to prove our medical fitness now, when we'd already been the parents of these children for more than two years?

Amit got on the phone with lawyer. She was unruffled. 'Just forget about it,' she said. 'I'll handle it – you just get the certificates for the children, that should be enough.'

Suddenly, our lawyer really did feel like a friend. And to think that I'd ever felt that she was adversarial!

We were nervously awaiting Dr S's arrival from about 10 a.m., but it was close to 3 p.m. when he finally rang our doorbell. By then the kids were asleep, which was just as well. Hardly had he seated himself and mopped his brow, than Dr S launched the first salvo.

'This asthenospermia,' he said, peering at some papers and stumbling on the long word, 'you know this condition is reversible, right?'

I was just about to shoot off an angry reply, when I remembered our lawyer's advice and kept my peace.

'So, what if you happen, God willing, to have biological children in the future?' asked Dr S. 'You are only thirty-six, you have another ten years ahead of you.'

I smiled serenely and answered that if it happened, we would be very happy.

'Yes, but do you have any real evidence of this condition,' he asked. 'Do you have the actual test result? I don't see it here – this is only a certificate from some doctor. This doctor is not even on our panel of specialists,' he said, looking sceptically at the medical certificate.

'It's from one of the biggest hospitals in Bangalore,' said Amit.

'It's always better to have more evidence,' Dr S countered. 'Tomorrow, if you should have your own child, and if something should happen to these children, you should have a good answer.' He looked up from his papers and smiled weakly at both of us.

If our lawyer had not warned us beforehand, the interview would have ended right there. If 'something should happen' to our children? What exactly was he trying to say to us?

Our guest, it transpired, had several other missiles in his armoury as well. He questioned the wisdom of my going back to work after I had spent two years at home as primary caregiver to our children. 'Normally, we don't allow the mother to go back to work until the adopted child is at least five years old,' he said.

'Allow?' My blood was already boiling, but I quietly assured him that the children were well taken care of. So then, he moved on to questions about how serious we were about the future of our children, asking for evidence of bank accounts in their name. I let Amit handle that one. We knew well enough how much of our thoughts were directed towards ensuring our children had a financially secure future. To be asked for evidence of it was only a mild insult after all we'd already put up with.

Before leaving, Dr S fired one final salvo. 'Most adopted children will go back and look for their biological parents at some point when they grow up,' he said, gulping his tea noisily. 'Many adopted children even move the court to release their papers from the agency and sometimes they even manage to track down their biological family. But in their case, it is very difficult. They were abandoned at the hospital itself, which means the mother must have made up her mind and she would have given a false address; hospitals don't ask for any proof of identity. So they will never be able to find out their real parents. In such cases, we advise that you should never ever even tell them that they are adopted.'

Another noisy gulp followed this alarmingly bad piece of gratuitous advice, while I considered the many ways in which I'd like to cause him bodily harm.

'Are you blind?' I wanted to ask him. 'One look would be enough to tell anyone that they are adopted – or else to cast grave doubts on my marital fidelity.'

But I had been forewarned, so I just bit my tongue and let Amit do the talking. He deftly sidestepped the issue, and enquired whether Dr S would like another biscuit.

After an hour or so of politely insulting us in our own home, Dr S took a quick look around the house, including a five-second peek at the sleeping girls, then he pocketed his fee and left.

'I was afraid he'd want to wait till the girls woke up,' I said to Amit as we closed the door behind him. In fact, I'd have expected him to want to talk to the girls – at least a little. Wouldn't that be the best way of finding out if they were healthy and happy? From all he'd actually seen of the kids, they could have been some other kids altogether, or drugged and comatose, or dead; he wouldn't have known the difference.

He'd asked us to collect a whole lot of supporting documents and send it to our lawyer in time for the hearing on Tuesday. Amit hurriedly called the lawyer and told her what had transpired. She listened grimly and dismissed his demands for more documents as frivolous.

'Just send me the medical certificates for the kids, that should be enough,' she said.

And so, Dr S went out of our lives, leaving me with a bad taste in my mouth. For the sake of our daughters, for the sake of our family, we would put up with even this.

I chanted to myself like a mantra, 'one step closer; one step closer...'

III

The hearing scheduled for Tuesday the next week didn't happen. It was pushed out by a week or two. Eventually, our lawyer told us it was done and we had a date for the next hearing: 1 April 2010, April Fools' Day. It was a Thursday and a good date for the hearing, because the kids' school had already closed for summer holidays and the next day was Good Friday, so we had a long weekend attached to it. Having visited Pondicherry seven times already (not counting a short holiday in Pondicherry, long, long before the adoption process), we weren't terribly enthusiastic at the thought of making a holiday out of this trip. But a long weekend was welcome all the same; it would help to take some of the pressure off. At least we did not need to get back to Bangalore in a hurry. We planned to spend Friday driving back at a leisurely pace, and we'd still have the full weekend in hand – to celebrate.

There was every indication that this would really be our last trip to Pondicherry. At this hearing, the judge would hold our 'enquiry' and pass a verbal order, agreeing to our submission. After that, it was only a matter of a little more time and a little more paperwork – or so our lawyer said.

'I'll only breathe easy when I have the papers in my hand,' said Amit.

I was holding my breath too. Ours was a simple case – there were no contentious issues and nobody was contesting our case. But you just never know. A few days ago, I'd heard a horror story from someone closely associated with the ACA in Bangalore. A child had been with a family under foster care for a year and a half when the case came up for hearing under GAWA. The judge – for no apparent reason – denied the petition. The child was taken away from her adoptive family and placed with another family.

I thought about the agony of the family who lost their daughter; the trauma the little girl faced in being suddenly taken away from the only family she knew and plonked in the middle of another family; and the predicament the new adoptive parents found themselves in, trying to bond with a four-year-old who would every day have made tearful, heart-rending demands for her 'other' parents.

The thought of it made my blood run cold.

'If any such thing ever happens to us, I will do whatever it takes to make sure nobody takes our girls away from us,' said Amit. 'I'll do absolutely anything.'

And so we set out a little before 5 p.m. on Wednesday afternoon, hopeful, but more than a little anxious. We were driving ourselves this time, with the kids strapped into the back in their car seats. We reached Thiruvannamalai around 10 p.m. and stopped for the night. The next morning we started early and reached our hotel in Pondicherry at 8 a.m. That gave us just an hour to look respectable, gobble up our breakfast and get to the lawyer's office.

The lawyer ran Amit through a series of questions. Most

of it was routine stuff, like date of birth, date of marriage, employment, income and so on. Then she asked him the twins' date of birth and the date of the GAWA, something we had never paid much attention to. Amit is not very good with dates at the best of times, and with the numbers 21, 25, 27, 28 being appended at random to the months February, June, August and October, he was quite nervous by the end of it! He noted everything in his cellphone and did some last-minute rote learning on the way to the court.

'I'll also have to ask you to testify that this is your sterility certificate,' she said at the end. 'It is one of the mandatory questions. I won't ask you any details about it, but you do have to say that this is your certificate.'

Amit nodded, still focusing on the dates.

'The judge might also ask you some questions, you have to answer those. In the end, I'll ask you what your prayer to this honourable court is.'

Amit looked blank. 'That we want to be named as the parents of these children,' he ventured, tentatively

'No, no,' she said brusquely, 'you have to say that you humbly pray that...'

Before we could recover from the shock of 'humbly pray', a flood of legal and sophisticated words flew past both of us without either of us catching more than a syllable here and there. Amit nodded mutely and then it was time to go.

We reached the courthouse two minutes after ten and

spent the next two hours waiting. Trying to keep the kids suitably still and quiet in the hallowed corridors outside the courtrooms was a stressful and impossible task. Eventually, I took them down to the lawn in the courtyard, while Amit and the lawyer waited in the courtroom. I had just got the kids comfortably settled in the shade, with a big bag of colour pencils and a couple of drawing books, when we were urgently summoned upstairs. I scrambled around on all fours, trying to retrieve the colour pencils and stuff them back in the bag, while also coercing the kids to get organized and come with me. I rushed upstairs – only to spend another tiring forty-five minutes trying to keep the kids under control once again. The slightest sound from either of them brought forth angry men and women from various hidden doors and cubicles, all intent on shushing every little squeak out of the two little girls.

Around noon, our lawyer told us we could go. 'Be back here by 1.15,' she said. That gave us just an hour to get back to the hotel, have lunch and come rushing back.

Between 1.15 and 2 p.m., we continued to wait. Amit said there was some heated conversation in court, but much of it was in Tamil and he wasn't sure what it was all about. It didn't look good, though.

Finally our lawyer came out and spoke to us. There was a problem.

'Ten days ago, he has received a fresh set of guidelines regarding adoption cases. It states that adoption under

HAMA must be filed by the agency, not the adoptive parents. He was about to throw the petition out,' she said.

Amit told me later that she had actually had a long and loud verbal duel in court with the judge. 'She was practically shouting at him,' he said.

'I told him that my petition is as per the legislation and he cannot throw it out,' explained the lawyer. 'So in the end, I agreed to amend it in some way and he has agreed to that.'

Problem solved? Apparently not.

'As per the new guidelines, you have to furnish a complete set of documents to the court for HAMA,' she went on. 'It's almost the same set of documents that you submitted to the family court for GAWA.'

'But we already got those documents back from the family court,' I interjected.

'No, we didn't get all the documents. We got only a few documents from the family court, not the original reference letters and other original documents that you submitted.'

'So which documents do we need now?' asked Amit.

She drew up a list. 'You might have to go back to ACA Bangalore and ask them to give you the original application for adoption,' she said.

Go back to ACA and get the original adoption application form? That didn't sound feasible. Would they be able to find it – it was almost three years ago! Besides, would they even *want* to go and look for it?

'He has agreed,' said our lawyer, 'that if you can get all

the documents, he will hear your case next week itself. Not on Monday, but probably on Wednesday.'

We went back to the hotel hot, tired and thoroughly dispirited. Initially, we wondered whether Amit should go back to Bangalore and work on the documents, while I stayed on in Pondicherry with the girls. At least it would spare them the long drive back and forth. But in the end it just wasn't worth it – there were a full five days between now and the next hearing, and two of those were working days.

We packed our bags and resigned ourselves to yet another 'last' trip to Pondicherry.

IV

There is probably no place on earth I'd want to visit nine times in two years, but if there were such a place, it certainly wouldn't be Pondicherry. Any journey, however mundane, usually excites me – any journey is an opportunity, an adventure – but not this one. I geared up for my tenth trip to Pondicherry without the slightest trace of enthusiasm.

We'd spent the intervening days rushing around collecting documents at a feverish pitch. Once again, we approached friends for reference letters testifying to our ability to be good parents. This time, it wasn't even remotely fun – it was mildly embarrassing and profoundly tiring. We printed the letters ourselves, and went around apologetically collecting 'autographs'. We printed out an enormous set of papers testifying to our financial status, our employment, our health, our identity and dates of birth and marriage, and made three sets of everything: one for the lawyer, one for the agency and one for us.

Luckily, we found that we had kept a copy of our original adoption application, so that was one headache less.

On Tuesday afternoon, we set off on the long drive again. Amit was almost falling asleep at the wheel, but we did the drive in one stretch, finally checking in to our regular hotel around 1 a.m.

Tara had fallen sick on Saturday, with a viral infection called hand, foot and mouth disease. She wasn't terribly sick, but she clearly wasn't well. The lawyer, when she heard of this, said that I could stay in the hotel with the kids in the morning. 'He will pass over your case, it's sufficient if you alone are present,' she said to Amit. 'Let them come in the afternoon, when your case is heard.'

That was a relief. The kids and I enjoyed a leisurely morning in the hotel, while Amit handed over the documents and rattled off the dates he had been memorizing. By 11 a.m. he was back. 'We have to be there at 12.15,' he said. 'The judge will hear our case at 12.30.'

It was around 12.40 p.m. when the judge wound up some other case, took a break, and returned to turn his attention to the adoption cases. There were two cases, and the other family's case was called first. Sitting right at the back of the large courtroom with several fans whirring, I couldn't hear anything of what was said, but got the impression that much of it was in Tamil. While the man was in the dock, the wife took the daughter and left the courtroom. I didn't want to do that – this was our case, I didn't want to be outside while it happened. I was hoping desperately that the girls would be well behaved and really, really quiet, so I could stay inside and hear everything.

Sister Rosemary from the agency went to the witness stand, and we were told by the lawyer's assistant to go and sit up front right behind the witness stand. So when things turned ugly in the other family's case, we had a ringside view, though most of the discussion was in Tamil and we didn't understand too much. It appeared that the Sister should have brought some papers with her, which she had neglected to do.

The lawyer suggested that the sister, who stays nearby, be allowed to return with the documents on some other day, but that the parents and child not be required to return for that session. That seemed fair to me – our part was over. The judge, apparently, didn't think so. He kept saying, in English, 'You are troubling your clients,' and waving in our direction.

That was ominous. Troubling us? He hadn't even heard our case yet. It already sounded like he was going to send us away and ask us to come some other day. We watched the proceeding with bated breath and sinking heart. I really didn't have the energy to go away and come back a week – or even a month – later.

It seemed to take ages, but finally the Sister was asked to leave the stand ... and we were called! Amit sprang up and rushed to the stand, thrusting Tara at me. Bad move. Tara tended to be 'daddy's girl' and to be thrust away in this undignified fashion in this hot, sweaty, unfamiliar courtroom when she had been comfortably ensconced in his lap for the past half-hour was utterly unbearable. She fussed and cried and fretted, and tried to follow him into the dock. A court official peremptorily picked her up by the waist and hand her back to me. Twice. The second time, she started wailing with such determination that the same court official ordered me out of court. The lawyers all turned to look at us. Some of them signalled to me to get out of the courtroom.

I didn't care. This was our case. I shushed Tara as best I could and kept my seat. Amit's 'testimony' (if you can call it that) was proceeding systematically. He swore to tell the truth. Then he was asked his name, date of birth, date of marriage, wife's name and date of birth, his job, his salary, his wife's job and salary, whether or not we filed tax returns, the children's date of birth, date of the GAWA decree, and so on. He answered each question with only minor fumbles. With each question, he was required to nod at the certificate testifying to it and, where applicable, show the originals. One by one, the entire set of documents we'd worked so hard on, was sent up as evidence.

At last the lawyer asked him what he wanted of this court. Luckily, she actually phrased the answer for him and all he had to do was to say yes, which he did extra loudly, so nobody could miss it. Then his part was done, and he came to where we were sitting, and Tara at once climbed into his lap and began to cheer up.

Sister Rosemary was on next. Apparently, the issue with the previous case was not applicable to us. Our lawyer later told us that with our combined income being so terribly high, the judge had been very suspicious that we might have paid the agency something extra to get our children. So she had already approached the Tamil Nadu ACA and got a letter from them stating that we had been contacted through the Karnataka ACA. This proved that we had not contacted the agency directly, so it was unlikely that we had been given any special preference or been asked for any extra payment.

Sister Rosemary, when Amit spoke to her later, was very candid about it. 'Nobody wants to adopt twin girls and then have to pay double the dowry later,' she said. 'The dowry system is very strong here. And on top of that, they are so dark. Even dark-skinned couples want a fair child,' she added, shaking her head sadly. She had twenty-odd children in her agency now, and 700 parents on the waiting list. Yet, three couples had rejected our twins.

'Thank god for that,' I thought. 'Thank god, our girls came to us.'

Sister Rosemary testified in Tamil – I gathered it had to do with the child study reports and our application for adoption. It was about 1.40 p.m. when her part was done and we left the courtroom. We conferred with the lawyer. 'Yes, it is all done,' she said in a matter-of-fact way. 'You'll get the verbal order after ten days, and then you have to put in a request for as many copies of the written order as you want. Each copy costs Rs 300. When that comes, I will courier it to you. You don't have to come back again'

It was just another day's work for her, but for us, the magic words were 'you don't have to come back again'.

The whole process of legalizing the adoption had been a long, long journey. At the end of it, there was no jubilation, no elation. Two years and so many trips to Pondicherry later, the only thing we felt was a huge sense of relief.

It would be strange to no longer have a trip to Pondicherry looming, a month or three down the line.

It would be a relief to know that our kids were now, at last, legally ours; that nobody could take them away from us; and that even if we both were to drop dead suddenly, they would be our heirs and would at least be provided for financially.

It would be a big moment some day in the future, when

we looked back at the day that our family finally became a legal unit.

But just then, it was like a huge bubble of tension that had been slowly growing for months, years, went pop … leaving nothing but a bit of spray and a big empty space.

ELEVEN

The Good Life

I

As soon as our girls came home, our lives changed radically. This, I'm sure, is inevitable for any couple that has led outgoing, footloose lives for many years before having kids. Where we once used to just hop onto a passing bus and head out of town for a quick, crazy weekend away, our trips away are now few, carefully planned, and involve plenty of preparation and lots of luggage. Where our weekends often had us leaving home before breakfast and returning well after midnight, we now tend to make short two-hour forays from home, always returning in time for the kids' meals and nap. And where meals themselves were usually ad hoc affairs, I now found myself racking my brains every day to think of wholesome, nutritious food that includes several types of fruit and veg for each meal.

The biggest change for me was giving up my professional life. While I did not quit *because* of the adoption, once the kids came home, I knew that it would be a long time before I went back to a working life. I'd always known that when we had kids, I would stay home for some time and just be with them; but I'd never been able to say with any degree of certainty what that 'some time' might be.

When we knew we were going to be adopting, I realized that 'some time' might actually be quite a long time – maybe even six months or a year. This was because I was anxious that initially I, or we, be the primary caregivers for our adopted child. I felt it would be easier for an adopted child to settle down in her new environment if she had only one set of people as parents and caregivers. Putting her in any kind of day care – whether home-based or outside the home – would mean introducing her to two new sets of people, and perhaps two different environments as well. That might be confusing or worrying for her, and might also slow down the bonding between the child and us, her adoptive parents.

As the months went by and the twins settled down and I got used to them, their needs, their personalities and so on, I began to miss my professional life. Was I really cut out to be a full-time, stay-at-home mom? The role felt quite constrictive. I was confined to the house almost all day long and all my time, energy and thoughts were child-centric. The 'me' that I had been used to seemed to have been completely replaced by this new me, who was forever thinking of the next meal and the next diaper change, and whether that runny nose was going to go away or turn into something serious.

This conflict was exacerbated by the fact that we had twins. I sometimes thought that if we'd had only one child, I might have tried to venture out more with her. But with *two* toddlers to manage, I couldn't even go out to buy some groceries and walk back with them.

I wanted to be with my kids, I wanted so much to make up for the time I had lost, that whole first year of their lives. I wanted to see them grow up, to watch their development and take pride in their every achievement, their first steps, their first words and all of that; but was that all I could be any more? Was there no way I could also have a little bit of the old 'me' back?

II

Soon after the twins turned two, and after I'd been a stay-at-home mom for over a year, I put them into the nearest and most convenient playschool I could find. It was a decision partly based on my selfish but genuine need to get some time off, and partly based on the observation that the twins were now ready for a more social life, where they could be managed by other adults and could interact with and observe other children.

The playschool I picked was a five-minute walk from home. It was a small, informal affair, functioning out of what was designed as an apartment in a housing complex. There were two teachers, two helpers and about twenty-five kids between two and four years of age. Whenever I saw it, it was noisy and chaotic, but it also looked reasonably safe and fun.

The first several days, I was asked to bring the twins for only twenty minutes or half an hour. The first day, I was allowed to sit inside while they found their way around. For the next few days, I waited outside. Within the first week or so, both had settled down at playschool and would leave my hand and go inside quite happily. Tara, in fact, was quite happy about her new environment right from the start; Mrini, predictably, had been clingy and upset the first couple of days, and one day she cried inconsolably inside, while I sat outside and felt my heart getting twisted in knots. But the next day, she only cried for a brief moment, and soon after that, she was as happy as Tara to go inside and came out half an hour or forty-five minutes later, smiling.

Soon, they were attending playschool for the full two-hour session, from 10 a.m. to noon.

What a relief it was for me! At last, I had some breathing space, some time to myself. It was hard to believe how desperately I needed to be away from the kids and how I treasured those two precious hours of freedom. I felt almost guilty at wanting so desperately to be away from the very kids I had longed so desperately for. But being closeted with two toddlers around the clock every day of the year is exhausting for anyone, even (or especially) for the mother.

From then on, things were never as bad as they had been in that first year. At last, I had a slightly 'normal' life, where I could read the newspapers, have a bath, cook, eat breakfast, or have an intelligent conversation on the phone – all crammed into the two hours when they were at school, or into the two hours of their afternoon nap. I could use the morning hours to run errands outside the house, which was a huge advantage. I could even begin to exercise regularly – something I'd completely given up on in the past year.

Meanwhile, as the kids enjoyed their preschool thoroughly, Amit and I began to think about school admissions. We were both inclined to the Montessori method over the traditional kindergarten approach. But Montessori schools took kids at two-and-a-half years of age, and Mrini and Tara were now already two years old. We hadn't known that, depending on the school's policy and the child's month of birth, you might have to start seeking admission into Montessori schools when your child is eighteen months old!

We applied to several schools around September–

October 2008. We didn't have their birth certificates at that time, so we always mentioned in a letter that, as our twin daughters were adopted and the legal process was ongoing, we did not yet have their birth certificates. In one case, we even had to explain that we could not have applied for admission the previous year, as suggested, because we had got the twins only at the end of September last year.

Of the several schools we applied to, two granted admission right away and a third called us for an interaction which, in that institution's admission process, implied that admission was more or less through. A fourth called us for interaction, which was routine and was done for all applicants, but then never got back to us. And a fifth just never responded to our application at all. To me, it sounded about par for the course. None of the schools we visited showed any special interest in the fact that our girls were adopted, although one of the schools did mention that they had several adopted children in their classes already. Nobody made a big deal about us not having their birth certificates.

One of my criteria for selecting a school had been, very firmly, that the school must allow the twins to be in the same section for as long as we, the twins and the school itself deemed advisable. I was quite worried that the school would insist on separating the twins, and it seemed very clear to me at the time that this would not be in their best interests. It was an enormous relief when Sishu Griha, the school we finally decided to admit them to, responded very cordially to my question around this. 'We let the parents of the twins decide,' they said accommodatingly. 'If we can see that it would be better this way or that way, we do advise the parents, but we don't insist on it.' The school was very highly spoken of by many people, seemed like a small and warm place, and had a very pleasant and sensible interaction. It was a little further from home than was ideal, but we decided that – all things considered – that was a small price to pay.

After attending their playschool for several months and then enduring the summer holidays at home with the greatest impatience, the twins joined their new school when they were a little short of three years old. They were right at home in a couple of days. Within a couple of months, they had got over all their initial shyness. Their teachers dubbed them the 'Toofan Mail'. 'They are both so naughty,' their teacher told me laughingly one day. 'The moment I turn my back, they start climbing up the walls. And the moment I open the door, they both run out and go straight into the sandpit.'

I took it – and it was intended – as a compliment. I thought back to how they had been two years ago, when we brought them back from Pondicherry in the car and parked them at home – small, sick, listless, scared, unmoving, weak and scarred. To see them running, laughing, shouting and driving their teachers to despair was joy beyond words. It filled me with a warm sense of great achievement.

If school admission had been easy, getting their passports was another story. It wasn't that we intended to go abroad for even a short vacation right away; we just wanted to get the paperwork done with. So we filled up the forms, ticked the box for adoption and attached the adoption deed and birth certificates. The only problem was that the adoption deed did not have a photo of the child – as per the passport office guidelines, this was required. Our lawyer said it would be difficult to get the photos onto the deed. The passport office said it would be difficult to get the passport without it. Even with it, they said, police verification would be required in Pondicherry as well as in Bangalore, just to be sure. It would take time.

Our friends had got passports for their children with no hassle and in a very short time.

For the first time since we started the entire process, I felt discriminated against. Why this extra process now? We weren't criminals, we weren't into child trafficking. We had faced everything – we'd been assessed, evaluated, tested, inspected under a microscope, examined by a judge, snubbed by a district magistrate, inquisitioned by a social worker – wasn't it enough? After we'd been through it all and passed, did we really have to go through one more round of questioning, explaining, defending?

In the end, the passport office settled for a letter from

the agency, with photos affixed. Several weeks later, we had the passports. The term 'adopted' wasn't mentioned anywhere in the document. Hopefully now, at last, we were at the end of more than three long years of paperwork.

III

By the time we got our twins, most of our friends had had kids as well. So, inevitably, our social life changed. The late evening outings to pubs, or to catch the late show came to an end. More often now, we met at each other's houses, where the kids could run around and play largely unsupervised. Evening get-togethers tended to wind up early, because 'the kids have school tomorrow'. Or sometimes even because 'the kids will wake us up at 6 a.m. tomorrow even though it's Sunday (groan)'.

Birthday parties changed too. Earlier, we had a gala party on Amit's birthday, when we invited all our friends home for a home-cooked meal preceded by plenty of alcohol and usually followed up with (home-made) chocolate cake and ice cream. Now, it was all about the kids. Many parties that Mrini and Tara were invited to were at fancy locations at malls or clubs. We continued to celebrate their birthday at home, but it soon became evident that that was the exception, rather than the norm.

In the early days, it wasn't easy to go out much with the kids. But by the time they were close to three, we could take them on a long tour of malls or to friends' homes, and they would last out the whole day, eating whatever came their way, forgoing their afternoon nap and then collapsing with exhaustion as soon as they got into the car to go back home at night.

We had been avid travellers before the kids came, and it was the one thing that we both wanted to get back to as soon as we possibly could. Apart from several road trips to Pondicherry, within the first year itself, we took the kids to Delhi, Chandigarh and Kolkata to meet family, and also to Lakshadweep, Binsar and Kasauli just for a holiday. Some of our long-distance journeys were by air, others by train. In February 2009, I even travelled from Delhi back to Bangalore by air alone with both of them, because Amit had returned to Bangalore a couple of days earlier.

It wasn't easy travelling with the kids, and it wasn't even always fun. There was a lot of planning, a lot of worry and a lot of responsibility involved. There was some guilt too. For instance, when we drove up to Binsar, a hill station in Uttarakhand, both the girls were terribly carsick for the entire duration of the three-hour drive. I felt miserable for putting them through that discomfort purely for our selfish pleasure.

And yet, I'd say that they generally enjoyed Binsar. We

took them for a long walk in the forest, where they pointed out various places where Snow White might have been lost when she saw the house of the seven dwarves; they wore wonderful warm clothes, jackets and shoes; they saw mountains; and they saw snow for the first time.

Some holidays were less pleasant than others. When we had gone to Kasauli, near Chandigarh, some months earlier, they had fallen sick on the way down. At first we thought it was carsickness, but the sickness persisted and worsened alarmingly by the time we reached Chandigarh. With two terribly sick little girls, we took the train from Chandigarh to Delhi and, a couple of days later, a flight from Delhi back to Bangalore. All four of us lost a lot of sleep and more than a little weight in that entire traumatic experience. It would be hard to say that the brief holiday in Kasauli had been 'worth it'.

On the other hand, we spent almost a week going to the Lakshadweep Islands. We went to Kochi by train, spent a day in Kochi, then boarded a ship to the islands. We visited three separate islands in Lakshadweep over the next three days, returning to the ship each night. We had long boat rides between the ship and the island each day, and one day we went on a glass-bottomed boat. The spectacular coral and the beautiful multicoloured fish made a lasting impression on both girls, especially on Mrini. As a result of this holiday experience, the girls now firmly associate 'boat' with 'ship' with 'island' with 'Lakshadweep' and with 'fishy-fishy'. They watched us go scuba-diving, and even ventured, warily, into the sea themselves. They had great fun with co-passengers on the ship, with bunk beds in our cabin and with sand on the beach.

As a family holiday, Lakshadweep was most definitely worth it. Our next ambition is a Himalayan trek – a short, easy trek. I'm sure my girls can handle it now.

As they grow up, everything becomes that little bit easier than it was some months ago. When they were in diapers, we had to carry diapers with us and find a place to change them when required. When they were being toilet-trained, we had to be able to get them to a toilet in a matter of minutes, or even seconds. But now those worries are behind us and we know they can manage a few hours at a stretch without needing a toilet break.

Food-wise too things are easier. They eat on their own, and ask for what they want and clearly refuse what they don't want. They can stand a fair bit of flexibility in what they eat and when they eat.

And though they generally still nap in the afternoons, they can miss it once in a way without any ill effects.

We can't yet go back to our completely footloose ways of the pre-kids days, but it now looks as though even that might follow soon enough.

IV

In retrospect, I know that opting not to work for more than two years after we got the kids was the right decision for me and for us. I know that if I had tried to go back to full-time work outside the home earlier, it would have torn me apart. I would not have been able to do justice either to my work, or to my family. So, though it wasn't always easy, and it wasn't always fun, I know that it was the best thing to do.

My rewards came in unexpected ways. There were so many magical moments of parenting that would lose their meaning in the telling, but were so very precious when they happened. I tried to recognize each such moment when it happened, to hold on to it and cherish it and keep it with me for a long, long time ... but like a ray of sunlight, it would leave me with a soft, warm feeling and glide away.

After more than two years away from the workplace, I finally resumed my career. The girls were settled at school, so it was just a matter of finding a good day-care centre and getting them settled there. They adjusted quickly and easily, much more quickly and easily than I could have hoped for. It was proof, if proof were needed, that they were confident, secure, happy kids, with no apparent scars from the early days of their lives. It wasn't easy for me, juggling home, family and work, making time for everyone and remembering to have fun – like any other nuclear family.

That was the wonderful thing: we were just like any other family now. If the girls have any psychological scars left over from their very early days, they are now completely hidden under silky black hair, smooth, dark skin, sparkling eyes and naughty smiles.

How could I ever think that they were not beautiful?

V

I have a confession to make.

Even though the endless yearning to have a child that I'd experienced in the years we spent trying to conceive was by now almost completely gone – to the extent that when Amit proposed expanding our family by adopting a boy, I quickly and firmly said no – the hurt and disappointment of not ever having been pregnant still lingered in unexpected corners of my heart. I didn't feel it often, not even once a year, let alone once a month, but occasionally, when I wasn't particularly thinking about it, it would come home to me surprisingly sharply: I will never be pregnant. I will have morning sickness, never see my body swell up, never have to worry about natural versus C-section, never – never – nurse a newborn. I will never experience any of this and I will never get to talk about it or even be able to share in the conversation when other women talk about it.

And other women, unfortunately, do talk about it – quite a bit, in fact. Less than a year after I went back to work, I had to suffer through an exquisitely detailed account of a colleague's pregnancy and labour-room story.

You're probably thinking: Oh my god, this woman is still going on about that. She's got her babies now, hasn't she? Why is she still whinging and whining about not having been pregnant?

The thing is – it isn't a big deal, really. I love my children just the way I would if they had been born to me the usual way. This has nothing to do with that. If I had ever given birth to any children I would have wanted them to be these very children; I can't even imagine any other children being my children. I firmly believe that these are the only children that were meant to be mine. Somehow or other, they had to come to me – to us. The slight, niggling regrets that I still have are unrelated with the joy, pride and satisfaction I feel in my family, now whole, now the way it was meant to be.

I don't grudge people the happiness and expectancy of pregnancy (any more). I don't blanch at the sight of pregnant women. I don't wonder (any more) when it's ever going to work out for me, or if, or how. I don't go home and cry – I can just go home and hug my kids and scold them (of course) and try to tell them how much I love them.

And yet, you can't take this acceptance for granted. If you rub my nose in it, it still hurts, just a little. If I hear the gory details of a friend's pregnancy and labour-room experiences in graphic detail, instead of responding with sympathy, I might respond with a tinge of envy. It's not that I'm making light of their experiences, it's just a slight but deep-seated expression of regret for something that I'll never have.

I know that pregnancy is not something I'm going to experience ever in this lifetime, and I have made my peace with that, but that doesn't mean it doesn't hurt at all. If you pick an old wound hard enough, if you scratch it deep enough, you still can draw a drop or two of blood from it. It's not completely gone yet. Not yet.

VI

There was never any doubt in our minds that we would talk to our children about their adoption. It was not something we would ever attempt to keep from them – for various reasons. For one thing, their features and complexion are completely different from ours and it's only a matter of time before people around them start noticing and commenting on it. But, even if that were not the case, I would still have wanted to tell them, because you can't keep something that significant from your own children.

Amit lost his mother when he was four and his family thought it best not to tell him about it. It was several years before the realization slowly dawned on him, from things other people said. I've seen his pain, his struggle with that unacknowledged loss only at second hand – albeit a close second hand – and it's not something I'd want to see my children going through. And they will find out. From friends, family, well-meaning strangers and ill-intentioned classmates, and ultimately, from the wealth of legal documents associated with it all. They will certainly find out. There's only one right way for children to find out a painful truth about their family and that is to tell them yourselves, honestly, and as soon as you possibly can. Tell them before they can understand. Tell them before they begin to perceive it as something different from normal, before they begin to see it as aberrant and therefore undesirable. Tell it to them as a matter of fact, without any judgemental baggage. Or at least, try to.

Another reason it's impractical to hide the adoption from them is for medical reasons. So many medical conditions run in the family; for adopted children, that genetic context is lost. At their age, nobody asks if they have a family history of high blood pressure, or heart disease, or diabetes. But when Tara had an outbreak of eczema, inevitably the question cropped up: family history of asthma or eczema? For Amit and me it would be: nil. For our adopted daughters, the answer is: unknown. And that, sadly, is all they have to go on for the rest of their lives.

I have, so far, never shied away from talking openly

about the adoption with anyone. I still remember how it was when I needed to talk to someone. I think if I had talked to someone even earlier, the whole infertility saga might not have hit me as hard as it did. Amit thinks I go out of my way to mention the adoption. If someone asks me, 'Was it a natural delivery?' or 'Did it go to full term?' or 'How many minutes apart were they born?' – even if I happen to know the answer (yes, yes, fifteen minutes) I still say, 'Oh, they're adopted.' I do this because if someone assumes I gave birth to them, I don't want to validate that assumption. Sometimes people ask these questions as a roundabout way of asking if they are my biological daughters. I don't mind – it's a polite way to ask, all things considered. And as they grow up, I certainly don't want my girls to think that their adoption is something I try to hide or brush away.

By the time our girls were four or five years old, people would ask their questions in hushed voices with a sideways look at the girls. Our replies, comfortably within their earshot, would cause nervous glances to be directed at us.

'Do they know?' they'd ask us cautiously.

'Of course they know,' we'd say.

I'm always surprised when people tell us we shouldn't have told them, or that we should now try to avoid the subject. In fact, we met a family who had an adopted daughter a little older than our girls. When we airily mentioned something about the adoption in conversation, we encountered the familiar nervous glance. 'She doesn't know,' was communicated partly through alarmed eyes and partly through frantic lip-sync. The daughter in question was more than six years old at that point. I was worried: how on earth were they going to tell her now? Six is much too old. A six-year-old already has a certain perception of the world and her family and her place in it. To tell her now that her parents are sort of not exactly her parents the way other kids' parents are – to clarify that she did not exactly come out of her mummy's tummy but out of some other mummy's tummy ... at six, it would come as a complete shock. And beyond that age there is no right time.

We started talking to our girls about their adoption when they were a little over three. We were fortunate to have been gifted a book tailor-made for the purpose, called *Tell Me Again About the Night I Was Born*, by Jamie Lee Curtis. It told the story of adoption in a picture-book format intended for very small kids. From there, it was only a matter of telling our children that this was not just 'a' story, but in fact 'their' story. They loved to hear that story – in the pictures, they identified us, their parents, their grandparents and the whole extended family; they even visualized the first few days after they came home with us. The book provided the bare bones of their story – we filled in the details.

The children – for now – are happy to just hear the story. They have questions, but they are the simple, innocent questions of a five-year-old. They understand that we are not their biological parents – at various times, each of them has even said, 'I want to have come from your tummy' – but they have not started actively discussing the matter with us yet.

Emotionally, adopted children will probably have a few extra bridges to cross on their way through puberty and on to adulthood. There may well be questions, doubts, insecurity and a sense of rejection or loss. There may well be an unquenchable desire to find out about their biological context. There may well be – and I'm not looking forward to this part at all – accusations along the lines of: 'I can't expect you to love me/understand me, you're not even really my mother.'

How are we going to get through this? I don't know. But I'm sure we will. We're a family, after all.